DEATH IN LACQUER RED

Also by Jeanne M. Dams

The Dorothy Martin Mysteries

The Body in the Transept
Trouble in the Town Hall
Holy Terror in the Hebrides
Malice in Miniature

DEATH IN LACQUER RED

A HILDA JOHANSSON MYSTERY

Jeanne M. Dams

WALKER AND COMPANY

New York

First published in the United States of America in 1999 by
Walker Publishing Company, Inc.

Published simultaneously in Canada by Fitzhenry and Whiteside,
Markham, Ontario L3R 4T8

Library of Congress Cataloging-in-Publication Data
Dams, Jeanne M.
Death in lacquer red: a Hilda Johansson mystery/Jeanne M. Dams.
p. cm.
ISBN 0-8027-3329-8 (hc)
I. Title.
PS3554.A498D35 1999
813'.54—dc21   98-45223
CIP

Series design by Mauna Eichner

Printed in the United States of America
2 4 6 8 10 9 7 5 3 1

ACHNOWLEDGMENTS

It is incumbent upon a writer of historical fiction to make clear which parts are history and which fiction. The Studebaker family—Clement, his brothers, wife, children, et cetera—did, of course, exist, and their descendants are alive today. Mr. Clem's mansion, Tippecanoe Place, still stands proudly on its knoll. Since, however, it now houses a fine restaurant, and there are few records of its original furnishings or the use of various secondary rooms, I have supplied these details from my imagination. Many other homes mentioned in *Death in Lacquer Red* are also real and still in existence, including the home I have given to the Harper family (the real home, then, of the Ford family, and now the Oliver Inn, a lovely bed and breakfast), and Copshaholm, the Oliver mansion. Certainly the University of Notre Dame is still there, though both Father Andrew Morrissey and Father John Zahm, noted scientist, professor, and intellectual, have long since gone to their reward.

I have anticipated the development of Leeper Park by a

year or two, and have altered some other historical details for my own purposes, including the date of the Indiana Republican Convention and rumors about corruption in the police force. I know of no such rumors in fact; so far as I know, the South Bend police have always been held in very high regard. I have taken care, therefore, to give this particular force a fictional superintendent.

Where real people are concerned, I have tried to adhere to a strict chronology. I have, of course, put words into the mouths of people who really lived, not meaning to imply that they actually said anything of the kind. I *have* tried to keep their words in character, insofar as their characters are known.

Most of the active cast of the book, particularly the entire Harper family and all the servants in all the houses, are creatures of my own imagination. Little information about the real servants of the day is to be found, so although I have tried to make the household much as it might have been, in size and makeup, any errors in that or any other regard are mine, and are not to be blamed on those who have helped me with my research.

Their name is legion, and though I've probably missed somebody, I'd like to thank G. Burt Ford, Tom Zoss, Carol Bradley, Ed Talley, Dorothy Corson, the staff of the archives department of the University of Notre Dame, Merle Blue, Corinne Stoddard, Peggy Livingston, the staff of First United Methodist Church, Venera Monahan, and The Reverend C. Marcus Engdahl. Three people deserve particular and fervent thanks: John Palmer of the St. Joseph County Public Library, who turned himself into my personal research assistant; Karen Olsen, my longtime friend and a *Svenska*, who provided the Swedish dialogue for me as well as valuable details about the

Swedish outlook on life; and Keith Kirkwood, manager of Tippecanoe Place Restaurant, who took me on an exhaustive tour of the huge house and showed me even the scariest cellars.

Of course, all the events of this book (except for certain incidents of May 30, 1900, and the Boxer Rebellion in China, about which you can read in any encyclopedia), are entirely fictional.

Finally, *Death in Lacquer Red* is dedicated to those historically minded men and women of South Bend who have labored so tirelessly over the years to preserve our heritage.

DEATH IN LACQUER RED

PROLOGUE

NORTH CHINA TERRORIZED
Bands Organized to Destroy the Homes of Christian
Converts—Works of Pillage and Murder by Boxers—
Would Drive Out Foreigners—Suspicion of
Government Connivance

> —*The New York Times*,
> April 15, 1900

T hank you, Hilda. That's very well done." Mrs. Clement
Studebaker smiled in her mirror at the maid hovering over
her shoulder, and patted a last curl into place. Her comfortable, round face was not made for beauty, and at her age she had
ceased to concern herself very much about such things, but her
hair must be properly dressed for an evening out, especially an
evening with Mrs. Harper, who was such a stickler for the social
niceties.

Hilda, for her part, breathed a silent sigh of relief. As head housemaid, she was not accustomed to such duties, but Michelle, the ladies' maid, was in bed with a cold, so Hilda had been pressed into service at the last minute. She blessed the hours the Johansson sisters had spent experimenting with each other's hair. "T'ank you, madam." She had almost obliterated her Swedish accent, but it surfaced when she was under stress. "Is dere anyt'ing else?"

"No, my dear. You may go and see to Mrs. George now. I must say, my daughter-in-law will repay your efforts better than this old lady." She smiled again, somewhat ruefully, and Hilda hesitated at the door.

"I t'ink you look very nice, madam," she murmured, and beat a retreat before she could be accused of overfamiliarity.

Left to herself, Mrs. Clem affixed a pair of diamond earrings to her ears, then sighed. All this fuss over a simple dinner with the folks next door! The older she grew, the more impatient she became with the demands of society. Needs must, however, when you were the wife of one of the richest, most important men in town, and lived in Tippecanoe Place, one of the biggest, most important houses. Mrs. Clem had always tried to do her duty, but to a girl raised on a farm, the forms duty took sometimes seemed a little strange.

As she sped down the hall to Mrs. George Studebaker's room, Hilda was thinking along similar lines. She, too, had been raised on a farm, though in Sweden, and in far greater poverty than any Mrs. Clem had known or imagined as a girl. She and her sisters and brother, the four eldest of the family, had come to America with dreams of bettering themselves, though Hilda had never imagined that by the year 1900 she would be living and working in the finest house in South Bend, Indiana. (Hilda's pride and loyalty allowed no suggestion that there might be any finer.)

But two hours to help two women prepare to eat dinner? She was fond of her employers, who were pleasant people, and considerate of their servants, but her private opinion was that the ladies had far too little to do. In two hours she could have dusted all seven of the principal reception rooms of the house and had time left over for some gossip with her friend Norah, the family waitress.

In due time the ladies were both ready, very fine in their silks and their jewels. Mr. Williams, the English butler, helped the two gentlemen into their coats and silk hats; Hilda slipped soft cashmere cloaks over the ladies' evening gowns, taking great care not to disturb their hair. Though they were walking only as far as next door, the early May evening was cold; spring was very late this year. The party set off, Hilda walking decorously behind the family and trying to remember exactly what duties were expected of her throughout the evening.

Michelle, lying feverish and miserable on her bed, had tried to explain. "I am sorree that you must work on your afternoon out, but I cannot do it. *Ma foi*, how I ache! The work, it is not hard, except for *les coiffures*. After *les dames* are dressed and ready, there is little to do. You will accompany them, and help them with their cloaks, yes? And make sure the hairs, they are all in place, if they have become *dérangés* by the wind. You will take the smelling salts, in case they become faint, and a fan."

"Must I stay with them all the time?"

Michelle sank back on her pillow, exhausted. "*Mais non*, of course not. You will stay in the hall outside the dining room, so that you will be nearby if you are wanted. And do not let that cook treat you as her free help. You are there to assist *les dames*, not the cook. Ah, go now. I will make it up to you."

Hilda nodded sharply. "*Ja*, you must rest, Michelle. Do not worry. I will do all that is needed." I hope I will, she added, but not aloud. Nervous though she was, she had no intention of admitting it to Michelle, who thought far too much of herself.

The moment she entered the Harper house, however, she began to relax. Though she saw the house from outside every day, she had never before been inside, and she saw at once that while it was a fine house, it was not nearly as imposing an establishment as Tippecanoe Place. For one thing, the door was answered by Annie, the housemaid. The Studebakers would never have allowed such a thing, no matter how busy the butler was. As for the family—oh, they didn't begin to measure up.

Not that Mr. Harper wasn't important in his own way. A tall man with iron gray hair and a stoop, he was the most respected judge in town and a big man in the Republican party, the party in power in the city of South Bend as well as most of northern Indiana and, of course, Washington. He greeted Mr. Clem and Colonel George with a firm handshake. Hilda, who had seen him only from a distance, thought he looked imposing, though nothing like as handsome as Mr. Clem, whose flowing white beard made him look like God. She was not at all impressed with Judge Harper's wife, who was short, thin, and sallow. Her face bore the lines of habitual ill temper, and she whined when she talked. Annie had told Hilda that Mrs. Harper came of a moneyed New England family, but she didn't look it. Her dull black gown fought with her complexion and hung on her stiff, spare figure in depressed folds. Hilda sniffed—inaudibly.

The grown-up children weren't much better. Oh, the daughters were pretty enough in clothes far finer than their mother's—too fine. Mrs. Reynolds, who lived on the other side of Tippecanoe Place, around the corner on Taylor Street, wore royal blue satin, sapphires, a few extra pounds, and a haughty expression, while her husband in his conventional evening clothes looked bored and uncomfortable. Mrs. Stone, from just down the street, was bony, shrill, and vastly overdressed in a draped and beaded and brocaded pink affair that might have come straight from Paris. Hilda didn't notice her husband; he was that kind of man.

As for the son, James, who still lived at home, he looked like a petulant, spoiled boy, though Hilda knew he was really in his twenties and an attorney in his father's old law firm.

It was a small dinner party. If you didn't count the colorless young lady who had obviously been invited to keep James entertained (and was apparently failing to do so), there were only two other couples as guests. Hilda heard the men introduced as partners in the law firm, but didn't catch their names. Though they were presentable enough, they were not to be compared with the national and international luminaries who often graced Mr. Clem's table.

As Hilda helped her ladies with their few needs, she looked unobtrusively about her. The house was certainly far less grand than Tippecanoe Place. To Hilda's trained eye, the signs of shabbiness and poor maintenance were evident. The velvet draperies were a little rubbed, a trifle faded. A picture hung slightly askew; there was dust in a corner. With her duties completed for the moment, Hilda entered the kitchen (smaller and less elaborate than the one she was accustomed to). She began to feel quite smug. This was nothing more than a very nice big house. *Her* employers lived in a mansion. She nodded and smiled condescendingly at Annie, who sniffed and gave her a sour look.

Hilda didn't even try to talk to the servants; they were run off their feet. The cook was rushed and nervous and therefore irritable. Her only helper, besides Annie and a waiter hired for the evening, was a girl named Wanda who spoke mostly Polish and was plainly terrified of the cook. Mindful of Michelle's warning, Hilda sought refuge elsewhere.

The evening, as it wore on, became increasingly boring. Hilda spent most of it sitting in the hall feeling superior, somewhat lonely, and hungry. She would really rather have helped out in the kitchen, but to do so would have violated the strict protocol that placed ladies' maids, even acting ones, above such duties. At least she could hear the table conversation quite clearly through the velvet draperies that curtained off the dining room doorway, but there was little of interest in the talk. Neither of her ladies required her attention, and she began to feel she had been brought along only because it was the thing to do.

In the hot, stuffy, and overdecorated dining room, as course succeeded rather tasteless course, Mrs. Clem was also bored and wondering why on earth she had come. Oh, she knew why, really. Duty called. But when a woman was approaching sixty, surely she was entitled to a spurious headache now and then. She would very much rather have enjoyed a quiet evening at home, eating one of Mrs. Sullivan's excellent meals from a tray in her room, and perhaps sitting down later with Clem and putting the final touches on plans for the new church they were going to donate to the Methodists of South Bend. She toyed with the idea of a fainting fit, but as she picked up her crystal goblet of water, she caught Clem's eye across the table. There was a twinkle in it. He knew what she was thinking; he always knew what she was thinking. He winked at her. She winked back and turned graciously to her host, at whose right hand she was sitting in the place of honor.

"I understand your sister will be returning soon from China, Mr. Harper."

"We hope so, Mrs. Studebaker. We have heard nothing from her since a letter arrived some three months ago. She said then that, with the Boxers becoming more and more active, the situation was becoming unsafe. She planned to leave by the first available ship. However, I understand that it has not been at all easy for foreigners to obtain transport, and, of course, a letter saying she had firm plans would probably travel by the same ship as she. I am hoping she will send a telegram as soon as she reaches San Francisco."

"Oh, dear. You must be quite concerned."

"Indeed. Of course we did try, the last time she came home, to tell her she would be safer here, but she was determined to go."

"It is noble work she is doing," said Mrs. Clem soothingly. "You can be very proud of her."

"Hmph! I tell her charity begins at home, and there are probably just as many heathen right here in South Bend who need their souls saved as there are in China, but she won't listen. She never did listen to me, even as a girl—stubborn, willful—"

"Rhubarb cobbler, madam?" The waiter proffered a dessert Mrs. Clem detested, but the diversion was welcome.

The meal ended, as all ordeals finally do. Mrs. Clem watched her hostess desperately for the signal that it was time for the ladies to retire to the drawing room while the men had their port and cigars. It would be the worst time of the evening for Clem, a teetotaler, but Mrs. Clem was panting for the chance to stand up. Her stays were cutting into her.

But Mrs. Harper remained seated, her eyes fixed on her plate and an expression on her face that would sour milk. Instead, their host stood and cleared his throat somewhat portentously. "With the ladies' permission, I am going to depart from tradition tonight. I confess that I have invited you here tonight, my family and my closest friends, for a purpose."

Closest friends, indeed, thought Mrs. Clem. She would have snorted if she hadn't been a lady. The only thing the judge and Clem had in common was their politics. Clem was certainly a staunch Republican, but that wasn't enough to make the two men friends . . . she jerked her thoughts back to what he was saying.

She hadn't missed much; the judge, like a true politician, was making the most of his opportunity for a speech. ". . . of course, is known to you all as the leading Republican, and the leading industrialist, in our fair city." He bowed to Clem, who gravely inclined his head. Only his wife saw the irony in the gesture.

"And of course my partners, or perhaps I should say, late partners. Though that makes them sound dead, doesn't it?" Feeble laughter. "When I was elected judge of this circuit court and gave up my law practice, Tom Hill and Jack Brookins remained to run the firm, and I am proud to say that they took as a partner, only last year, my son, James, who bids fair to become, someday, as good a lawyer as they are."

There was a polite little spatter of applause. Mrs. Clem sipped her water and eyed young James over the top of the glass. He emptied his own glass, which had not contained water, and gestured imperiously to the waiter to refill it. Well, the partners could hardly have done anything other than take the boy in, if he wanted to be a lawyer, or if his father wanted him to be—which amounted to the same thing—but he'd do better to stay away from so much wine if he intended to follow in his father's footsteps.

"And finally my dear wife and daughters. I—er—I am afraid that my giving up the practice meant considerable sacrifice on their part." The judge began to sound a little less expansive. He glanced at his wife nervously. She sat with lips pressed into a firm line and transferred her gaze to the wallpaper. "I—that is, I have had far less time to spend with them, and there is—er—the financial aspect of abandoning a good practice. Of course, my fine sons-in-law have been a prop and a stay, both for me and for the ladies of my family."

Said sons-in-law had moody expressions on their faces and

avoided looking at each other or at the judge. Mrs. Clem again caught her husband's eye; he twinkled briefly at her. They would enjoy talking about this when they got home.

"At any rate, after long hours of meditation and, I may say, consultation with those honorable members of our party whose advice I so value, I have come to a momentous decision, and I have called you here together tonight so that you may all know what it is. I must tell you that the information I am about to impart is not yet public knowledge, and must not be made so for a few weeks yet. I'm sure I need have no anxiety in that respect."

He took a deep breath. "Ladies and gentlemen, family and friends, I plan, on May thirtieth, Decoration Day, to announce my candidacy for the United States House of Representatives!"

The waiter had been primed for that moment. He moved swiftly around the table with filled champagne glasses. Mr. Clem, for whom the announcement had come as no surprise, rose, glass in hand. "This is an auspicious occasion, indeed. I propose a toast, ladies and gentlemen, to William Harper, the next representative from the Thirteenth District!" He raised his glass, touched it to his lips, and put it down untasted. Mrs. Clem, who had guessed what was coming thirty seconds into the speech, did the same, thinking as she did so that Judge Harper, though a reasonably good politician, was going to have a hard time defeating the incumbent, Abraham Brick, for the nomination. Mrs. Harper did not even lift her glass; she, as Mrs. Clem recalled, was the sort of teetotaler who strongly objected to anyone else enjoying wine either—or enjoying much of anything, for that matter. The two daughters, looking more unhappy than jubilant, took decorous sips, not looking at their mother; the sons-in-law and partners drank heartily, and son James drained his glass.

In the hall, Hilda, who had heard every word, sat up with a yawn. They would go home soon now, she hoped, and after she had gotten the ladies undressed and ready for bed she could get some rest herself. At least there would be something to tell the other servants in the morning; the Harpers had lost a lot of their money and the judge was moving into important politics. That should stir some interest. Not that it made up for losing her afternoon out.

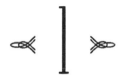

The flowers that bloom in the spring, Tra la,
Breathe promise of merry sunshine—

—W. S. Gilbert,
The Mikado, 1885

"ell, look at that, will ye!"
Hilda turned her head from contemplation of some ducks that were bobbing their heads in the water, tails jutting ridiculously into the air. Her companion, Patrick Cavanaugh, sat in the bow, oars shipped, the rowboat drifting idly near the riverbank under the shade of a huge maple tree. His finger was fixed on a page of the newspaper that had wrapped their now devoured sandwiches. Hilda glanced at it, saw nothing of interest in the columns of fine print, said "*Ja, ja*," in lazy fashion, and returned her attention to the ducks.

"All right, then, but listen to this," said Patrick. "It says here there's going to be an opera at the Oliver Opera House, next month, for a whole week. It's called—oh, dear, the—the *Mick-a-doo*, it must be. But it's by Gilbert and Sullivan, and they're grand. When I was a boy and lived near Dublin, one of their shows came to town once, all about a sailor and an admiral, and everyone was singing the songs . . ."

He saw that he was losing Hilda's attention and switched his tactics. "I'd like fine to see this one, and I've got a little money put by for something special. What would ye say if I asked ye to come to the opera with me?" He twirled the ends of his luxuriant handlebar mustache and fixed his brilliant blue eyes, with their thick black lashes, on her face in a practiced, soulful gaze.

Hilda snorted, apparently immune to his charm. "I would say that you had lost your mind. Patrick, you dream. Operas are for rich people, not firemen, or servants! When would the two of us have time or money to make holiday in the evening? Even if it were allowed, which it would not be, not without a chaperone. The Studebakers are fine people, I do not say different, but there are rules, and Mr. Williams, he is very strict, *ja*. He would never permit me out with you in the evening." Some devil made her smile coyly and add, "Unless—if we—if I and you—if it was understood . . ." She lowered her eyelashes with maidenly modesty and then suddenly opened them wide to catch Patrick's look of alarm.

Her laughter rang out; the boat rocked with her mirth. "Oh, Patrick, if you could see yourself. You look like a herring! Your eyes, they bulge!" She composed herself. "Me, I should not talk so silly. Me and you—it is not possible. Me, a Swede, and you an Irish Catholic! Our families would—" Her English, good as it was, wasn't up to describing the probable reaction of both families to the idea of an engagement. "So," she said firmly, "we are friends, and the day, it is beautiful. Let us enjoy it."

It was, indeed, a perfect May afternoon. The cold, wet spring had given way to sudden hot weather, and all the flowers had bloomed at once. The riverbanks were covered with wild phlox or, where houses and lawns were established, with fragrant lilacs and lilies of the valley. Oaks and maples and huge, magnificent elms stood proud, their limbs lush with soft new green leaves that stirred dreamily in a gentle breeze; the golden willows dipped their delicate fronds in the river. The sun shone bright and hot.

Here, where the river made a sharp bend, the south bank was low and flat, covered with grass and dandelions, but to the north, the river was confined by a steep, brush-covered crag. Hilda, cool in her best white muslin, lay back against the cushions that Patrick had provided for her comfort. Feed bags they might be, stuffed with hay from the firehouse barn, but they were soft and smelled sweet, and she could pretend they were the silken pillows of the rich. "What is that church, Patrick?" she asked, looking upward. "It is a church—*ja?*—with the cross on the—it is not a spire, I do not know the English word, the round—"

She pointed, frustrated, to the structure, atop the crag, that could just be seen from their low vantage point.

"Oh, the dome," said Patrick, squinting into the bright sky.

"That is what a dome is? Then that is, perhaps—"

"It's the church at St. Mary's Academy."

"Oh," said Hilda, disappointed. "I do not know this St. Mary's. I thought it was perhaps Notre Dame. That, I have never seen, but I have heard people say it has a dome."

Patrick laughed, a rich laugh of comfortable male superiority. "Not a piddlin' one like that! St. Mary's, that's the girls' college, run by the nuns. Not," crossing himself hastily, as though the feared Sister Mary Bridget of his childhood were listening, "not that they're not good, holy women. But, Hilda me girl, you've never seen the likes of the dome at Notre Dame. It's on the main building, not the church, and it's solid gold, mind, with a statue of Our Lady in gold on the top. Ah, 'tis a fine place, Notre Dame. That's French for 'Our Lady,' you know."

Hilda, conscious of being condescended to, sniffed. "I know that it is very silly to spend much, much money on a gold statue when so many people are hungry," she said flatly.

For ye have the poor always with you, Patrick started to quote, and then thought better of it. In a year's acquaintance he had learned that it was safer not to get into a discussion of religion with Hilda, who had strong views on that subject, as well as most others, and whose beauty was equaled only by her stubbornness and her temper.

Hilda, sensing both his temerity and his admiration, preened herself. She knew Patrick was sometimes a little—not afraid of her, exactly, but wary, and she enjoyed the knowledge. She was also pleasantly aware that she looked her best today. Mrs. Clem and Mrs. George were generous with gifts to the servants of their outmoded clothes. The white muslin skirt and waist were beautifully made and embroidered, and Hilda had laundered and ironed them lovingly, mending one or two tiny rips and tears so skillfully that no one, she was sure, could tell. There was a blue sash to go with them, and a fine straw hat with blue feathers, nearly as good as new, that flattered her oval face and golden coronet braids.

But her interval for flaunting finery and playing the lady was drawing near its end. The sun was well into the western arc of sky; afternoon was advancing. She sat up. "Patrick. We must go back. I must change into the uniform before we eat our supper. And your work, it will be hard, to go up the river."

Patrick sighed and removed his jacket. It was all too true. The St. Joseph River, despite its placid appearance, had a current that, in spots, was the very devil. If it had carried them pleasantly and easily downstream, rowing upstream would be a hot, back-breaking business. He seized the oars, turned the boat around, and made for Leeper Park.

Hilda studied him covertly, admiring the play of muscle against his shirt sleeves. She wasn't entirely sure why she enjoyed Patrick's company so much. It was true that he was a good-looking fellow—and knew it, too, she thought with a private grin. And he could spin a line of talk to turn any girl's head, any, that is, except the hard, sensible head of a *Svenska*. Then there was his fiddle, a treasured family relic that he had brought from Ireland and could play with a rollicking lilt that reminded her of barn dances in her village back in Sweden. But everything else was against it. Their backgrounds were entirely different, save that both came from grinding poverty in the Old World. Their religious differences struck sparks, from time to time. For that matter, many of their conversations struck sparks; both had passionate opinions and volatile tempers. That was probably the root of the attraction, she admitted with another inward chuckle. It was such great fun to argue with Patrick!

And what was the harm in an occasional afternoon out? Especially if her sisters didn't know.

LEEPER WAS THE newest park in South Bend, and the most fashionable. Patrick was showing off by taking Hilda there for boating instead of to the older, more democratic Howard Park, just above the dam. Leeper Park was for the gentry. On this lovely spring afternoon it was crowded with ladies in beautiful pale dresses, hems sweeping the grass, elegant parasols raised to keep the sun off their faces. Their arms rested on those of dapper gentlemen in lightweight tweed suits, striped shirts, high collars, and straw boaters. One sporty gentleman in bright-yellow checked knickerbockers had a bicycle, one of the popular safety bicycles with equal-size wheels, and was trying to persuade his companion to try it. She was dressed for it, too, in a divided skirt whose calf-length hem shocked Hilda, and natty little boots up to the knee, if one's imagination were bold enough to go so far. Hilda spurned the attempt. Ladies, in her opinion, possessed limbs, not legs, and certainly neither calves nor knees. Her eyes lingered on the bicycle, though. They were all the rage, and Hilda desired with her whole soul to own one, even while knowing that such a thing was utterly out of the question. To ride one, perhaps, someday . . .

The squeal of a child caught her attention, and her throat was suddenly tight. The boy, about six, she judged, had somehow escaped the surveillance of his nursemaid, and was dirty and disheveled and having a glorious time. He reminded Hilda so of her youngest brother, Erik. He'd been about that size when she'd last seen him, three long years ago. He would have changed a lot. How many more years would have to pass before she would see him again? She sighed deeply.

"What's the matter, me darlin'?"

"You must not say things like that," Hilda replied automatically, but her mind was still on her family. "I think of how long it will be to save enough money."

Patrick didn't have to ask enough money for what. He and his brothers had gone through the same long, grinding effort to bring the rest of their family to America. Four men, working long hours, had been able to do it in half the time it would take Hilda and her sisters. There was the brother, of course, working at Studebaker's; he must be a big help.

"You'll do it, me girl," he said with comforting warmth, and pulled the boat in to the shore.

The man who rented the boats helped Patrick tie up at the

landing and handed him out of the tippy craft, but Patrick insisted in lifting Hilda out himself and setting her, with long skirts still dry, on the pier. His hands lingered around her waist perhaps a fraction longer than was strictly necessary.

"Enough of that," she said sharply. "There was no need to fetch me out like a parcel. I have the use of my own feet."

"And such pretty feet," said Patrick, unrepentant.

Hilda snorted, and set a brisk pace across the park. Patrick gave the cushions to the boatman, to be fetched later, and then continued to linger a pace or two behind Hilda, enjoying the view. She had a neat little waist, set off nicely by the blue sash of her gown. Her skirt twitched beguilingly about her booted ankles as she strode across the grass, and one of the plumes of her straw hat drooped a bit, caressing her neck where a few enchanting strands of gold had worked free from the restraints of the braids atop her head. Patrick wished he dared emulate the bold blue feather.

She shook her head impatiently, brushing the feather away. "Do you see me home, or not? If you do, be of some use. I need help to cross this street; it is as muddy as— Patrick Cavanaugh, put me down!"

He did—on the other side of the street, and not before his lips had brushed her cheek. Hilda didn't speak to him again for many long blocks, not until they had traversed the whole of North Main Street and then of West Washington, and finally toiled up the steep back drive to Tippecanoe Place.

"Please—I'm sorry, Hilda." Patrick paused and put out his hand placatingly. "Will you come and sit for a little and talk to me?"

Hilda's indignation had largely dissipated, and she had no wish to go inside a moment before she had to, but it was necessary to keep Patrick in line. Still without a word, she crossed the back lawn to the bench by the carriage house and sat down, her back to Patrick, studying the tall hedge of white lilac that edged the back of the Studebaker property.

"I said I'm sorry! I won't do it again."

"No, you will not!" Hilda crossed her arms. "Such a thing—and on a public street! If Gudrun or Freya would see you, they would send me back to Sweden on the next boat."

"Your sisters are too old-fashioned," Patrick began, and Hilda turned on him.

"You will not talk about my sisters!"

"You talk about them," Patrick pointed out. "All the time. You say they won't let you ride a bicycle. They won't let you meet my family. They won't let you do anything that's—drat these flies!" He batted at the large insects that were buzzing drowsily about his head.

"That is different. They are my family and I can say anything I want—what is the matter?" For Patrick was frowning and sniffing the air.

"Someone's left some garbage behind those lilacs. All those flies—and can't you smell it?"

Hilda sniffed and made a face. "Ugh, yes. It will be the scullery maid, that Elsie. She is stupid, lazy—I do not know why she is allowed to stay." She stood. "I think I must clean up the mess before Mr. Williams sees it, though I should like to leave it for Elsie. Step out of the way, Patrick; I shall look."

"Hilda, no!" said Patrick in sudden awful apprehension, but she brushed off his restraining hand and swept around the end of the hedge, Patrick in pursuit.

The woman's body lay crumpled behind the lilacs, the late afternoon sun beating down upon it mercilessly. Hilda saw only two things, a bright-red silk jacket and the formless pulp where a face should have been. Then she grasped Patrick's arm and began to scream.

SOME OF THE NEEDS OF SOUTH BEND
... A complete garbage system with crematory.
—South Bend *Tribune*,
January 1, 1900

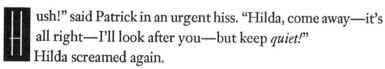ush!" said Patrick in an urgent hiss. "Hilda, come away—it's all right—I'll look after you—but keep *quiet!*"
Hilda screamed again.

"Hilda Johansson, if you bring the family out here with your hysterics, you'll lose your job, and probably mine, too!" Hilda took another deep breath. "Bless all the saints, here's Mr. Williams coming!" Patrick added hurriedly.

Hilda choked, hiccupped, and turned to look at the staircase leading up from the basement kitchen premises to the back porch. The kitchen door was shut; neither the butler nor anyone else was on the stairs. She turned a furious face to Patrick.

He ignored it. "There now, that's better, me girl. Now look here, Hilda, I've got to be gettin' the police. You get inside and tell Mr. Williams what's happened. I'll fetch your coachman—oh, here he is."

John Bolton came out of the carriage house, yawning and stretching. "What's up?" he said. Then he saw Hilda's face and looked at Patrick sharply. "What's happened?"

Patrick told him, in an undertone, his eyes on Hilda. She had forgotten her anger at Patrick's lie. Her face was even paler than usual; her breath was coming fast and shallow. Patrick watched her anxiously, torn between his civic duty and his chivalrous concern.

"Take some deep breaths," he urged. "Me mother says it's the best thing when you're upset. Can you get to the house all right, do you think?"

Hilda managed to nod.

"Then I'll leave John to watch over the—what's back there. I've a run to make. The nearest call box is on the Olivers' corner, by Copshaholm—or—would they let me use the telephone in the house?"

"I d-do not think so. The servants are never allowed." Her voice was steadier; her color was coming back. She was ashamed of her weakness. Death was no stranger to a farm girl; she had killed many a chicken herself, back in Sweden, and had assisted in the slaughter of many a pig. It was that face . . . she stamped her foot and directed her distress at Patrick. "If you will go, go! I must tell them, in the house!"

Patrick made for the front drive at a dead run and Hilda, following more slowly, started down the narrow stone steps to the kitchen door.

The kitchen was quiet. Hilda frowned. It was nearly five o'clock. At this time of day, dinner preparations should have been well under way. Neither Mrs. Sullivan, the cook, nor Mr. Williams was in sight. She tapped on the door of the butler's pantry and, receiving no response, opened it a crack. He wasn't there. Rows of delicate china and crystal glassware and silver serving pieces gleamed behind locked glass doors, but the work surfaces were bare and clean. No butler, no cook.

She found both of them, with most of the other servants, in the room next to the butler's pantry that the servants used as both dining and sitting room. It was a peaceful scene. The sun, this late afternoon, was on the other side of the house, but even in the semi-basement enough light still shone through the large window for Mr. Williams to read the South Bend *Times*. His bull terrier, Rex, snored at his feet. Mrs. Sullivan, in an old rocking chair, was knitting something intricate; her lips moved as she counted stitches. The kitchen cat, too old and too sleepy for direct action, watched with half-shut eyes as the twitching yarn unwound from the basket on the floor. Hilda's friend Norah and young Anton Weiss, the footman who came in by the day, were playing checkers at the table. Norah was beating Anton badly. And in an overstuffed chair that had seen better days, Elsie, the despised scullery maid, simply sat, her mouth slightly open.

Hilda cleared her throat.

"Ah," said Mr. Williams, glancing up and immediately returning his attention to his reading. "You have returned. I trust you had a pleasant afternoon with your young man?"

Mrs. Sullivan snorted. She did not approve of any sort of relationship between a Swedish Lutheran servant and an Irish Catholic fireman, be it ever so friendly and platonic.

"Mr. Williams," Hilda began, and stopped, extremely annoyed that she could not control the tremor in her voice. She cleared her throat and began again. "Mr. Williams, I—"

"What is it, girl? I am *attempting* to read the newspaper.

With the family going out this evening, there is time for a brief period of relaxation, and I—"

"Please, sir!" The tremor was gone, but the pitch had risen almost to a squeak. She lowered it. "Sir, I must speak to you."

He lowered his newspaper reluctantly. "Very well. I trust you are not planning to give notice. You would find it very difficult to secure as good a position anywhere else."

Hilda restrained herself with difficulty. She knew she must not interrupt him again. "No, sir. May I speak to you privately?"

"Nonsense! There are no secrets in this household. Out with it, girl."

Something in Hilda's voice, or her attitude, caught Mrs. Sullivan's attention. She looked sharply at the butler and opened her mouth, then shut it again. His word was law.

Hilda took a deep breath. "I did not remember that the family was going out. I thought I could find you alone and speak to you only, sir, but it is as you wish. Something terrible has happened. There is a woman on the ground, in the white lilacs. She has been murdered, and I found her body."

The reaction could scarcely have been more sensational if she had set off a firecracker under Mrs. Sullivan's rocking chair. Elsie shrieked and threw her hands in the air, pulling up the skirt of her apron to hide her face. Mrs. Sullivan dropped her knitting and sat up, her hand to her heart. The rocking chair tilted perilously forward, and the cat, whose tail had been under one of the rockers, yowled and tore across the room and up the fireplace to the mantel, knocking over a large vase on its way. Lilacs and water and broken china cascaded to the stone hearth, and Rex woke from his sound sleep and began to jump and bark hysterically.

"Rex, be quiet! *Down*, sir! Elsie, pull yourself together, girl, and clean up that mess! Anton, stop looking sick and make yourself useful. Capture that cat immediately! Cease this noise, all of you!"

While Mr. Williams shouted commands to which no one, including Rex, paid the slightest attention, Norah slipped around the table and put a hand on Hilda's shoulder. "Are ye all right, then?" she whispered under the din. "Horrible, it must've been, finding her like that. If ye like, I can run and fetch ye a nip of the cooking sherry while Cook's not looking."

Hilda gave her a grateful look, but shook her head. "There is no need. It was not pleasant, but I have recovered, I think." She giggled, a trifle hysterically. "They are like chickens in the barnyard, Norah!"

Elsie, cowering under the butler's fury, was attempting to mop up the water, but Rex, still excited, rolled in it and then shook himself vigorously, spraying water everywhere. Anton attempted to seize the cat on the mantel, who hissed at him, clawed his hand, leaped down, and retreated under the overstuffed chair, uttering loud feline profanity. Mrs. Sullivan, red-faced, stood shaking her fist in Elsie's face, berating her (most unjustly) for the breakage of the vase and the ruin of the lilacs, while Mr. Williams was reduced to futile gestures and anguished moans.

Upon this scene of chaos the door opened, and John Bolton walked into the room.

"I see you've all heard the news," he said with a grin, and sat down on a damp footstool.

Well, you get some repose in the form of a dose,
with hot eyeballs and head ever-aching,
But your slumbering teems with such horrible dreams
that you'd very much better be waking . . .

—W. S. Gilbert,
"The Nightmare Song,"
Iolanthe, 1882

The coachman's impertinence, on top of everything else, was more than Mr. Williams could bear. He clutched at the rags of his dignity, pulled himself up to his full height, and seemed to puff up. He reminded Hilda of the turkey cocks on the farm back in Sweden, and she stifled another nervous giggle.

"That will be quite enough of that, John Bolton!" said the butler. "You will remember your manners, sir. Remove your cap at once, and be so good as to go out and clean your boots before you return. If, indeed, you find it necessary to return. Surely you have duties to attend to."

It didn't sound like a question, but John took it as such. "They're all going out for the evening, *as* you know, but as it's only next door at the judge's house, they don't need the carriage. The horses are fed and watered and the stables are mucked out and the carriages are polished. You bet I'll be back; this is too good to miss!" As an outdoor servant, John was only technically under the butler's authority, and he took every advantage of the fact. He was careful to slam the door as he left.

Mr. Williams closed his eyes in momentary pain at the use of slang by a member of his household, not to mention the discussion of matters that should be kept to the stables, then opened them again and turned them accusingly on Hilda. It was clearly her fault. She was the one who had started this riot!

"Now, my girl, explain yourself and these unseemly hysterics. Norah, sit down."

Norah sat in the nearest chair, rolling her eyes heavenward as she did so. "*Whose* hysterics?" she whispered to Hilda.

Hilda privately agreed that, though she had good reason, she had indulged in no hysterics. Indeed, she was one of the few who had not. Looking at Mr. Williams's face, however, she decided not to argue with him. She *was* under his authority, and he could be very domineering when he chose. She did hold her back very straight and her head very high. If the butler had his dignity to maintain, so had she.

"There is little to tell. I and Patrick come up the back drive— he sees me home, you understand. We talk. And then we—" She paused, remembering all too clearly the flies, and the smell . . .

With a shaky breath, she continued, her face reverting to its earlier pallor.

"We thought it was some garbage someone had left there, and I went to look."

"Whatever made you suppose someone had left garbage behind the lilacs? I would hope everyone in my household knows better than to do such a thing!"

Hilda gulped. "I do not want to say, sir, if you will excuse. It is not—not very pleasant."

Mrs. Sullivan moaned gently, and Hilda hurried on, struggling to maintain her composure and her manners. "But it was a woman, sir. She lies there, dead, and her head—" She came to a stop again.

"A woman? What woman? And what makes you think she was—murdered, I think you said? What a preposterous idea!"

Her control snapped. "Oh, I cannot answer these questions! I do not want to think about it. I hope they will take her away and I shall never, never have to see her again. And you ask who she is—I say her own mother would not know her, and that is the truth. She has no face!"

That was too much for Elsie, who clapped a hand to her mouth and rushed for the lavatory. Norah swallowed hard, but remained steadfastly at Hilda's side.

Mr. Williams, for once, was silenced. Hilda lowered her voice and spoke more gently. "I am sorry to make everyone so upset, sir. Better I had talked to you alone. May I go now, and put on my uniform before the police—"

Mr. Williams found his voice again, and with it some measure of common sense. "Yes, you may go, Hilda. I see that your involvement with this matter is entirely accidental. I'm very sorry, I'm sure, that you have had such a terrible experience, and I shall see to it that you are not troubled about it, by the police or anyone else. The sooner we all forget this, the better."

Hilda could hardly believe her ears; she spoke before she

thought. "A woman is dead, Mr. Williams! Of course the police will talk to me, and to everyone in the house, it is likely. And I, myself, wish to know—"

"Enough!" thundered the butler. "It is not seemly for young women to wish to know about murder. If the police wish to speak with anyone, they may speak with me. You will not talk to them. Do you understand? You will not speak of this to anyone! Whoever this—this person was, the matter can have nothing to do with us! Now be off with you all— there is work to be done!"

He waved an imperious hand, and Hilda, biting her tongue, stamped out of the room, Norah close at her heels.

Hilda muttered all the way up the steep service stairs. By the time the two women reached the top floor, three stories up, she was panting and in a towering rage. She opened the door to her room and, flinging herself on the bed with a clash of springs, began to pull off her boots and hurl them across the room.

"He cannot tell me what I shall and shall not do!" *Crash!* A boot hit the wall. "If the police wish to ask me questions, I will answer them, *ja!*" *Clang!* The other boot ricocheted off the radiator and nearly hit Norah, who sat on the chair by the washstand, listening patiently. "And if I wish to speak to anyone, I will. This is America, a land of freedom! I am not a slave . . ."

She went on in that vein for some time as she changed into her black uniform, lace cap, and apron, and Norah waited for her to wind down.

Finally, with a sigh, Hilda pulled on her black stockings and secured their garters, buttoned herself into her thinner black indoor boots, and stood up.

"Are ye through pitchin' yer boots at me, then?" asked Norah.

Hilda studied her feet as though to make sure the boots were buttoned properly. "I am sorry, Norah. I have the terrible temper. I am still angry with Mr. Williams, but I should not have thrown my boots." She looked up at Norah. "Or at least—I should have been more careful where I threw them."

Norah barked a laugh. "That temper is going to get ye in trouble one of these days, Hilda me dear. That or yer curiosity. Or both."

TRUE TO HIS word, Mr. Williams dealt with the police himself. Hilda, once she had calmed down, was secretly relieved. She had nothing of substance to tell them, after all, and the police were not always kind to immigrants. Patrick had told her stories about their treatment of the Irish that had made her blood run cold. True, those things had happened years ago, and in big cities like New York and Boston . . . but South Bend, with over forty thousand people, was becoming a good-size city, and its police force was rumored to be less than ideal. Some said they took bribes from illegal taverns, in the form of supposedly confiscated liquor. Certainly it was a fact that a new superintendent had just been appointed, a man from out of town who, it was said, had been brought in to clean things up. But, new boss or not, it was also an undisputed fact that they would run a man in with far fewer questions if he was a Polish factory worker than if he was an American lawyer. Everybody knew that and took it for granted—even though Polish names made up a fair percentage of the police roster.

Stubbornness can be a curse. If she had been given no orders, Hilda would probably have been only too glad to try to forget that poor woman in the bright-red jacket. Or, at least, she would have been content to follow the story in the newspaper as best she could.

But Mr. Williams had told her she was to have nothing further to do with the matter, and her temper was roused. Who had a better right to find out exactly what had happened than she, who had discovered the body? Who was Mr. Williams to tell her what to do, and what not to do? Furthermore, she didn't need to await the pleasure of an inefficient and possibly corrupt police force. She could ask her own questions, thank you very much, and tap into that invaluable network, the servants' grapevine.

She finished her duties early; there was somewhat less cleaning to be done in warm weather. True, open windows let in more of the soot produced by the ever burning smokestacks of South Bend's many factories, but there were no ashes from the mansion's twenty fireplaces to deal with. Then, too, it was quicker and easier to clean a room properly when the family was out. Servants were not supposed to be seen going about their duties, and they certainly could not, under any circumstances, interrupt anything family members or their guests were doing in a room, no matter how inconvenient it was to let the chores there wait.

That warm May evening, by skipping the supper for which she had little appetite, Hilda was able to get the reception rooms and bedrooms in perfect order well before the family returned from their dinner party. She thought about skimping on Mr. Williams's room (all the other servants were supposed to clean their own), but prudence rescued her from that folly. She would give Mr. Williams reason enough for annoyance by her continued involvement in the murder; better not also give him reason to find fault with her work.

It was barely past nightfall of that long, near summer day when she fell into bed exhausted, but she found it hard to sleep. The other servants were later in coming upstairs, and until they settled down for the night there was noise—subdued, but irritating to her frayed nerves. She dropped into slumber when quiet finally descended, but woke after what seemed only a short time.

The room was airless and far too hot. She pushed the sashes up as far as they would go, cranked opened the transom that she had shut to keep out the noise, and climbed back into bed, where she tossed restlessly, hearing the clock far below in the great hall chiming the quarters.

When, at last, sound sleep came to her, it transported her not to rest, but to the world of nightmare. She was in a boat, it seemed, alone, drifting farther and farther from shore into the swift, deadly current. She shouted for Patrick on the riverbank, but he said he wasn't allowed to talk to her and turned his back. There were no oars, so she reached perilously over the side to paddle with her hands, but a woman swam up out of the depths of the river to try to pull her in. All Hilda could see was her back, as wet and sleek as a seal's, and her white, clutching hands. Then the woman turned her face up, but she had no face . . .

She woke bathed in sweat, her heart racing. Had she screamed? There was no sound of disturbance from the other servants' rooms, so perhaps she had made no noise. But there was something—some sound farther away—a little cry, almost like a child's—

There was no child in the house. Colonel George's son, Master George, was thirteen now, and away at school, in any case. Was—could there be something wrong with one of the family? Surely Michelle, who slept on the floor below, would wake and seek help if anyone were ill. But the sound—there it was again! More like a cry of vexation, and *not* from the top floor.

A burglar? Last night she would have said it was impossible. Last night she would have said murder at Tippecanoe Place was impossible. She got out of bed, her bare feet making no sound on the wooden floor, and pulled on her only dressing gown, a long, heavy woolen one. It was far too warm, but she couldn't go abroad in the house in her nightdress, even at such an hour. The hinges creaked as she eased her bedroom door open, and she cast silent imprecations on the head of the hapless Anton. He was supposed to keep the hinges oiled.

The top floor of the great house could be a frightening place even in the day, if the day were stormy. At night, it was terrifying. All the gas lamps had been turned off hours earlier, of course. (The mansion had suffered a devastating fire only a few months after it was built. Almost eleven years ago, that was, but everyone in the rebuilt house was still extremely careful about fire; the servants weren't even allowed candles in their rooms.) In Hilda's cramped corner of the house, back by the service stairs, there were no windows save those in the bedrooms, making the narrow hallway as black as the pit. If there *was* a burglar, the darkness was her friend, in a way, but she had to see *something*. The only solution was to leave her door open. The rising moon was on the other side of the house, but a little reflected light penetrated her windows, and there was a faint glow from the street lamp on the corner. It was better than nothing.

Not much better. The dark paneling, the dark doors of the storage closet that lined one side of the hall, swallowed up what little light there was. Her heart beating so loudly she was sure any possible burglar could hear it, Hilda crept past Norah's door and felt her way around a corner, out into the foyer of the great ballroom that dominated the top floor.

Here there was a little more light, shining through the tall windows that lined one side of the ballroom. Their shutters were folded back, their velvet draperies left open, their sashes thrown up to their fullest extent to catch any breath of air that might be stirring. Hilda stopped and listened. She could hear no sound, now, except for the regular snores of Mr. Williams, clearly audible through the transom of his large room on the east side of the house. Moving very carefully—it would not do to run into a chair

or a piece of statuary and wake him!—she tiptoed to the head of
the stairs leading to the family bedrooms on the floor below.

No sound. No strange, muffled cries. No indication of a
burglar or any other cause for distress. She felt her way down a
few steps, glad they were carpeted and solidly built so as not to
creak, until she turned on a landing and stood behind the elevator
that ran up the center of the stairwell. Then a few more steps and
another turn, and she was at the top of the short flight leading
down to the second floor.

Still nothing. No light, no sound, only the dark, enclosed,
breathing silence of a sleeping house.

A loud *whirr* and a clicking noise! Hilda clutched the railing,
her hand grown clammy with fear. She willed her heart to slow
its beating, tried to take a deep breath, and through her panic
heard three deep, solemn chimes.

Only the clock in the great hall, clearing its throat to strike!
Nothing more.

Ashamed and disgusted, she made her way back to her room.

The moon, a little higher now, and just past full, shone in
obliquely through her south window. She pulled off her dressing gown and stood at the other window, for propriety's sake.
She had no wish to be spotlighted by the moon in her nightdress, but she was desperate for some cooling breeze. There
was none. Perhaps if she knelt on the window seat and put her
head right out the window? Holding tightly to the window
frame, she leaned outside. Involuntarily, her eyes focused on
the white lilac hedge.

The hedge was a double one, lilacs on the Tippecanoe Place
side, well-trimmed privet on the side of the Harper backyard.
Between the two was a narrow space of grass and weeds, accessi-
ble only from the ends of the hedges to north and south. It was
here that Hilda and Patrick had made their terrible discovery,

and it was here that Hilda now, in the hard, bright moonlight, saw movement.

She thought at first it was a dog, nosing around the place where the body had lain, and she made a small sound of nauseated disgust. Quiet as it was, the sound was loud in the stillness of the night, and the figure straightened and looked around, then, as if satisfied it could not be seen through the thick hedges on either side, bent its face to the ground again.

Hilda, from her lofty viewpoint, saw only the twitch of a skirt on the grass. She did not stay to see whether the figure had a face. Tears of terror slipping unheeded down her face, she pushed frantically away from the window, exploded out her door, and beat frantically on Norah's.

"Norah! Wake up! Norah!"

Her fists made little sound on the solid oak door; her cries were little more than whispers, so breathless was her panic. Norah slept on, unheeding.

At last Hilda slipped back to her room, locked the door, pulled the covers over her head, and lay, whimpering, waiting for the morning light.

Early rising is indispensable if a servant would do her duty. . . .
—*The Practical
Housekeeper*, 1872

A hammering at the door brought her to reluctant consciousness.
"Hilda! Why ever have ye got your door locked? It's gone
five-thirty, and ye'll be late. *Hilda!*"
Muttering something highly improper in Swedish, Hilda
stumbled to the door and unlocked it.
"And would ye like me to bring ye up a breakfast tray, me
fine lady, so as ye can go back to bed and have yer sleep out?"
Hilda gave Norah a black look, then turned to splash cold
water on her face.
"La-di-da! Cat got yer tongue?"
"My tongue has no trouble," said Hilda coldly from the folds
of a rough linen towel. "It is yours that goes too fast. Now go. I
wish to dress."

Norah, in high dudgeon, marched down the service stairs carrying her lidded chamber pot and never so much as glancing back. Hilda sighed, yawned mightily, and set about dressing and pinning up her hair as rapidly as her foggy brain would allow.

It was going to be an oppressive day. The air hung heavy, still, and as hot, inside, as it had been been at its warmest yesterday. If there was fresh dawn air anywhere, it did not penetrate to her room. The morning sun shone bright and brassy, but to the south and west, her two views, sullen clouds were massing. There would be thunder before the day was out. Hilda sighed resentfully as she did up the many buttons of her high-necked, long-sleeved, long-skirted uniform. She had often suffered from cold in the drafty old farmhouse in Sweden, but she found the relentless, humid heat of Indiana much harder to bear. And it was not yet summer!

It was after six-thirty when, her early-morning chores completed, she entered the servants' dining room. The sun shone in through the one large window, for the room was only slightly below grade. "Basement" was something of a misnomer for the lower floor of Tippecanoe Place. Since the great house was built into the side of a small hill, the rooms on the east side faced a gentle slope, and the windows let in plenty of light in the morning.

Mr. Williams frowned. "You are late," he informed her. "The porridge is cooling."

She shuddered at the very thought of porridge on such a day. "I will not take any, thank you." She slipped into her place at the breakfast table. "Only toast. And coffee, please, Mrs. Sullivan."

"You'll have an egg," said the cook flatly, pushing a bowl of boiled eggs across the table. "Or two. You had no supper last night, and you look like the wrath o' doom this mornin'. Was it nightmares you were havin' in the middle of the night, then?"

Hilda looked cautiously at Mr. Williams, who had finished his breakfast and was smoothing out the pages of the South Bend *Times*, preparatory to ironing it and presenting it to the family. "I am sorry," she said, evading the question. "Did I make a noise?" The cook's bedroom was directly across from Hilda's, but Mrs. Sullivan usually slept like a hibernating bear.

"Not as I heard. But why would a person lock her door, unless she were affrighted?"

Hilda sipped her coffee, hot and strong, nibbled at some toast, and shot Norah a reproachful look. She had violated the unspoken code that they did not tell tales on one another. But Norah lifted her chin and turned away. "If I may be excused, Mr. Williams," she said, standing up without a glance at Hilda, "*some* of us have our work to do. *Some* of us can't sleep all day, with no thanks to those who try to help us, neither—"

Mr. Williams, with a red face and a stifled, choking sort of noise, stood up and pointed at the newspaper in his hand.

"Our neighbor!" he said in tones of shocked disbelief. "Miss Harper!"

"And what about our neighbor?" asked the cook.

"She's dead! Murdered! It was she who was found . . ."

He stopped talking, and his eyes, and the eyes of everyone in the room, swiveled to point squarely at Hilda.

"But how is it known who she is?" she cried. "Her face . . ." She shuddered, and Mr. Williams scanned the small print rapidly.

"Her clothing was identifiable, it seems. She was wearing a distinctive jacket, in a color called 'lacquer red,' brought with her upon her recent return from China. She is— that is, she was a missionary to the heathen there, as you will recall—"

There was a stifled cry from Michelle D'Aubray, and attention shifted to her.

As ladies' maid, Michelle had a very different schedule from that of the other servants. Busy helping Mrs. Clem and Mrs. George to dress when Hilda came in the day before, and then accompanying them to their dinner party and returning late, she had heard nothing of the excitement.

But she had her contribution now, and she made the most of her chance at the spotlight. She rose and clasped her hands dramatically to her bosom. "*Ah, mon dieu!* So that was the reason she did not appear for her dinner, *la pauvre demoiselle!* They were very worried, see you, *très dérangés*, her brother, her sister-in-law, when she did not come. For the dinner, it was in her honor, and they could not understand why she did not send word about her absence from her *soirée*."

If capturing everyone's attention had been her goal, she had accomplished it. She went on, letting her voice assume a low, thrilling timbre, and being a good deal more French than strictly necessary in accent and vocabulary.

"She had returned, *voyez-vous*, from China. But only last week! The rebels there, *les assassins*, they are killing the foreigners, the missionaries, even—"

"We all know that, Michelle," said the butler repressively. "The Boxer uprisings have been in the newspapers for weeks. Miss Harper had left her mission work in China as a result and come to stay with her brother, Judge Harper, for a time. That is not new information."

"*Mais oui!* She had come to be safe, had come to escape persecution, because here, here in the bosom of her family, she would be protected, she would be safe. But the terror, it followed her! It was here, here in this haven, with her loved ones, that she was struck down—"

"Strictly speaking," said John Bolton, who had finished his hearty breakfast but was delaying his work in order to enjoy the excitement, "it was not exactly in the bosom of her family that she was struck down, but behind our hedge. And what was she doing there, I'd like to know?"

Michelle made an airy gesture, annoyed at the interruption. "Behind our hedge! But that is absurd."

"It isn't, you know. Hilda found her there, didn't you, love?"

Hilda, who didn't want attention, could have strangled John, and so, by her expression, could Michelle, who did want it. Michelle shrugged and spread her hands. "'Ow would I know why she was there? She had been out all day, they said at dinner. There was some—some business she wished to conduct. I do not know. I only know that she did not come, and did not come, and they had to serve dinner without her, and Mrs. Harper, she was very annoyed, and the soufflé, it was ruined."

Mrs. Sullivan clucked and shook her head, apparently more at such wanton disregard of good food than at sudden death.

"But—how extraordinary!" said Mr. Williams, intrigued in spite of himself. "You mean to say they were giving the dinner for her, and then she wasn't there? Did anyone offer any explanation?"

Michelle preened, having recaptured the stage. "Judge Harper, he could not think of any reason, but his son, Mr. James—?"

Michelle paused interrogatively and Mr. Williams nodded. "Yes, yes, we all know Mr. James. What about him?"

"He is a lawyer now, *savez-vous*. He is in Judge Harper's old firm. He said that Miss Harper had said she would come to the office at some time yesterday, for this business, whatever it was. But she made no appointment, since it was in the family, and she knew she could walk in at any time. So Mr. James did not think anything was amiss when she did not come. He said—they all laughed, I remember—he said, 'She'll have run into one of her preacher friends, and forgotten all about dinner. Aunt Mary always did care more about God than her stomach.' You will forgive, Mr. Williams, my mentioning *l'estomac*, but it is what Mr. James said.

And all the time the poor lady was lying there, dead . . . *ah, mon dieu* . . ." Eyes upraised, she crossed herself solemnly, a gesture that seemed to embarrass the butler, especially when Norah and the cook repeated it (though with rather less dramatic flair).

"Ah . . . yes. Well." He cleared his throat. "It is all very distressing, I'm sure, and I must apologize for—er— mentioning it over breakfast. I was simply—ahem—rather startled by the account in the newspaper. No doubt there is some simple explanation for the entire incident. But I must remind you all . . ."

Hilda, who had been quietly absorbed in eating toast and eggs, put down her spoon. Mr. Williams, his own curiosity satisfied, was about to exert his authority again and tell them they were to have nothing more to do with this murder. Was this the time for her to speak? To tell him, as deferentially as she could, that she could not remove herself from this matter, that she intended to find out what had happened to this woman she had found so horribly mutilated? She took a deep breath and waited for the butler to finish his little lecture.

She didn't get the chance.

"Excuse me, Mr. Williams, sir. I—I am sorry, but—"

"What *is* it, Anton?" Mr. Williams rattled the newspaper, and the footman in the doorway looked even more terrified.

"I—there are people here who wish to speak to you, and to the staff, and to—to the family, sir—and—"

"To the *family*? At this hour of the morning? Have you lost your mind, young man?"

"Well, sir, they are the police, you see, and—and here they are!"

And Anton fled from the wrath to come.

A policeman's lot is not a happy one . . .

—W. S. Gilbert, *The*
Pirates of Penzance, 1879

There were three of "them," and they entered the room as if they owned it, or at least the first one did. A short, portly man with a red face and a mustache that bristled, he was clearly in charge, and intended that no one should make a mistake about that. Patrick had entertained Hilda one afternoon with a dissertation on the uniforms and insignia of the fire and the police departments. She didn't need the information to recognize the superintendent of police. He strutted.

Behind him was, Hilda thought, a sergeant. The third man was a mere patrolman, a young man who looked approachable. He was certainly the only one who did. All three were sweating in their blue woolen uniforms, buttoned to the chin.

"All right, now, who—ah. You!"

"Were you addressing me, sir?" Mr. Williams's tone was chilly in the extreme.

"Who else, man? Are you in charge here?"

"I am the butler, sir. I supervise the staff."

"Limey, ain't you? Well, you can climb right down off that English high horse of yours and tell Mr. Studebaker I'm here, and I want to talk to him."

"I regret that it will not be possible, sir."

"What do you mean, not possible! Do you know who I am?"

"No, sir. You have not introduced yourself, nor stated your purpose in coming here."

Hilda thought she heard a stifled laugh, but a sidelong glance showed her that the young patrolman's face was perfectly neutral, his eyes facing straight ahead.

The superintendent's face grew redder. "I'm Harry Clarke, superintendent of police. There's been murder done, man, and don't tell me you haven't heard about it! Don't be more of a fool than you can help; you go get Mr. Studebaker, and do it right now!"

Mr. Williams stood rigidly still, his face a mask. "It is, sir, still lacking some minutes of seven o'clock in the morning. The family have not yet arisen. You have not indicated which Mr. Studebaker you wished to see, but Mr. Clem is an elderly gentleman, and in indifferent health. Colonel George has been suffering from a slight indisposition for the past few days. I could not undertake to awaken either of them."

The butler's chin had been rising higher and higher during this stately speech, until he seemed to be addressing the ceiling.

"By God, I'll go wake 'em up myself!"

"Certainly, sir. If you feel that is the best way to ensure their cooperation and goodwill."

There was dead silence. Harry Clarke might not have lived and worked in South Bend long enough to be thoroughly familiar with the various members of the Studebaker family, but he'd been there long enough to know that they and the Olivers were the Powers in the Land. Though not a man of great intelligence or strong imagination, he could suddenly see himself storming into the bedroom of one or the other of the richest men in town—there would be a wife, presumably, in some state of undress—there would be screams, shouts—he would be asked to explain himself—

He took a handkerchief out of a pocket, pulled off his hat, and wiped his streaming brow.

"Drat it! I came all the way over here, myself, just to talk to—to Mr. Clem, I guess. By gum, I'd like to . . ."

He glared at Mr. Williams, who maintained his statue pose, his eyes still fixed on the ceiling. The butler's will was clearly as rigid as his bodily attitude. The superintendent capitulated, though with a bad grace.

"Nice for some people to sleep as late as they want! When *will* your precious boss be out of bed?"

Mr. Williams looked directly at him with a glacial eye.

"Er—that is—when will Mr. Clem be available?"

"I could not undertake to say, sir. His usual hour of arising has been modified somewhat owing to his ill health, and he was rather late to bed last night. He may have engagements, as well."

"Damn it, man, when do I come back? Ten o'clock? Eleven?"

"I could not undertake to say, sir."

It was a clear rout, but Clarke was not going to let the butler have it all his own way. "All right!" he said viciously to the sergeant. "You, Haney, stay here and get the story from everybody who *is* awake. You, Lefkowicz" (to the patrolman), "you stay as a witness. You might learn something. And don't either of you let any of 'em put anything over on you. I wouldn't put it past *him*. Foreigners!" With a final contemptuous glance at the butler, who had not moved, the superintendent strode out of the room, and Hilda saw the look he exchanged with his sergeant, the lifted eyebrow, the almost invisible nod.

In the strained silence he left behind, they heard an oath as he made a wrong turn in the backstairs labyrinth, heard his panting, labored progress up the steps outside the back door, and finally his snapped order to his driver and the clop of a horse's hooves down the drive.

The two policemen looked at each other. They were going to have to walk back to the police station.

Mr. Williams spoke.

"Did I understand the—the person who has departed—to say that he wished you to question my staff?"

Sergeant Haney, who possessed a little of the diplomacy that his superior so conspicuously lacked, hastened to pour some hypocritical oil on the troubled waters. He smiled and shrugged.

"I know it's a nuisance, Mr.—?"

"Williams."

"—Mr. Williams, but it probably won't take very long. Waste of time, if you ask *me*, but he didn't ask me, did he? I'll let you tell me who to talk to when, so it won't be quite so inconvenient."

"It is extremely inconvenient, young man. This is one of the busiest times of the day. I cannot possibly allow you to disrupt my household in this way."

"Would it be better if I just followed 'em around and talked while they work? I have to take back a report, you see, or it'll be my neck."

The butler allowed himself an ambiguous, wrathful noise. "It certainly would be most inappropriate for you to 'follow them around,' as you put it. You are not a guest in this house. You have no right to the freedom of it."

Sergeant Haney smiled, having won his point. "Well, then, I guess I'll just have to talk to 'em here. Who first?"

Grudgingly Mr. Williams conceded, realizing it would be less trouble in the end. "Very well, if you must, you may speak first to Anton and Michelle, so that they will be free to attend to the family when they awake. Elsie, fetch Anton. I don't know where he's gone, but he *ought* to be cleaning the boots. The rest of you, off about your business! The work of this house has not come to a stop because of an unfortunate incident. You will be summoned when you are needed."

Hilda stood, stiffly. She could not distinctly remember having breathed for the last several minutes. So this was what the police were like when they were engaged in their official duties! The superintendent was bullying, crude, ignorant—and bigoted, as well. He had not had the sense, yesterday, to look personally, searchingly, into the murder of an unknown woman. Even the fact that the body had been found at Tippecanoe Place had not stirred him to action. But now that the murder victim had become "important"—the sister of a judge—he was plainly slavering to arrest someone as soon as possible. She shivered, remembering his intonation on the word "foreigners" and his wordless understanding with the sergeant. The morning did not bode well.

She went, as ordered, into the kitchen to help Mrs. Sullivan with preparations for the day's meals.

It was stiflingly hot in the big kitchen. The fire in the huge cast-iron range was, of course, never allowed to go out. From the time Mrs. Sullivan came downstairs in the morning and stirred up the fire, to the time she went to bed at night with it damped down, it made the kitchen feverishly hot. The warmth was welcome on a cold winter morning, when the servants' bedrooms were distinctly chilly despite the central heating, but on a May day that might have been borrowed from July, Hilda could have done without the stove. Sometimes in summer Mrs. Clem would order cold meals and the stove could be damped early in the day, after everything had been prepared and set to cool in the big iceboxes. Today the calendar said it was still spring, so the family meals would follow the usual pattern. Eggs, ham, steak, pancakes, potatoes, doughnuts, bread, applesauce, stewed prunes, and so forth were Mrs. Sullivan's first concern of the day. Family breakfast was imminent, and so many things had to be done at the last minute.

There was no kitchen maid as such, only poor Elsie to do the most menial and unpleasant chores, so Hilda assisted at certain times. She was allowed no part in the actual cooking, of course, except when a big dinner party meant all hands to the pump. Then she might be asked to stir a sauce or test a cake. But on an ordinary morning, with the downstairs rooms clean and the bedrooms occupied, her job was to slice the freshly baked bread, fetch pots and bowls, supervise the scatterbrained scullery maid, and generally make herself useful to the harried cook. As soon as the family were down for breakfast, she would hurry upstairs to make the beds and tidy the bedrooms before the occupants returned. She was always rushed in the morning, always on edge. Today was worse then ever, with the heat—and the policemen across the hall. Strain her ears though she might, she could hear no word from the servants' room.

"If you're thinking that bread is to be served to the family," said Mrs. Sullivan grimly, "you'd best slice it thinner than that, and neater. We're not wantin' crumbs for the birds, you know."

"I am sorry, Mrs. Sullivan." She bent to the bread board, attacked the loaf fiercely, then gave a little cry and thrust her thumb into her mouth.

"And I'd thank you," said Mrs. Sullivan, without turning from the oven, "not to bleed on it, neither."

It was almost a relief when the kitchen door opened and Anton poked his head in. "He wants you now, Hilda."

Her handkerchief wrapped firmly around her cut thumb, she hastily smoothed her apron and followed the footman out of the room.

"Was it bad?" she whispered as they crossed the hall. "What did he want to know?"

"Not as bad as I was afraid it would be," Anton whispered back. "He is—not like policemen at home, in Prussia." There was no more time to talk. Hilda walked into the familiar room, suddenly grown unfamiliar and threatening, and stood, hands clasped in front of her.

"You are Miss Hilda Johnson?"

"Johansson," she replied, making it three syllables and giving the initial letter its proper Swedish pronunciation, like a *y*.

"Er—yes. Sit down, will you, Miss—Miss Hilda?"

She sat, her back, shoulders, and mind as stiffly rigid as the hard wooden chair. He might have been able to get round that snob of a butler, this policeman who despised foreigners as much as his superior did, even if his manners were better, but he wouldn't get anything out of *her*.

"Now I understand you found the body—oh, excuse me, you do speak English?"

"Certainly I speak English." She could hardly pull herself up any straighter, but her lips set in a firm line.

"Good," said Sergeant Haney, not appearing to notice the coolness in the atmosphere. "Then tell me about it."

"There is not something to tell. I looked, and she was there. They have told you how she looked, or you have seen, yourself."

"Now, Miss Hilda, I want *you* to tell me."

"I do not want to talk about it. It is not pleasant to remember. Especially," she added cannily, "when I am very hot and not feeling very well."

She suspected that the sergeant, sweltering in his uniform, might not be feeling too well either. Apparently he decided, for whatever reason, that it was wiser not to go into the physical details, for he passed on to another subject.

"Ah—yes, well maybe we can leave that for later. Now, just what time was it when you saw the body?"

Hilda's scorn grew. This was not as hard as she had been afraid it might be. "I am not a lady, Sergeant, not rich," she pointed out. "I do not have a watch, and I did not look at the kitchen clock when I came inside." He wouldn't know that a country girl, brought up on a farm, could tell the time of day by the sun. He thought foreigners didn't know anything. "I felt sick, in my stomach," she added, in case he had missed the point earlier.

She heard, once more, a sort of half sneeze from the corner where the patrolman was trying to be inconspicuous. Once more a quick glance showed her only a bland countenance, but she considered. He had a foreign name himself, something Polish, she thought. He knew. She was sure a moment later when he lowered one eyelid slowly, though he never looked at her.

"Yes, well, you'd been out for the afternoon, right? With a friend?"

Hilda's patience was growing thin. "You know that I was, Sergeant Haney. Mr. Cavanaugh was kind enough to rent a boat and take me out on the river."

The policeman guffawed. "Paddy Cavanaugh! I know him. Unlikely sort of friend for a Swede, eh? An Irish Catholic? And a fireman? Trying to start a fire, the two of you, are you?"

Hilda sat in stony silence. This was insufferable, but she

dared make no protest. Sergeant Haney scowled, running a finger around his tight, sweat-soaked collar.

He made one last try for some information. "Did you see anything at all that was out of the ordinary? Anyone where they shouldn't have been, anything like that?"

She tried not to let her expression change, but the memory of the woman in the night flickered across her eyes in spite of herself. Her tightly clasped hands never moved, though, and her mouth never relaxed. She was not going to tell them what might have been only a terrible dream. Or, if it had been real—

"I saw nothing, Sergeant. Nothing at all."

He tried to stare her down, but she had learned that art of stolid impassivity so necessary for a servant.

"You're lying," he said flatly.

It was not a question. She made no reply.

After a few more minutes of repetitive questions and monosyllabic answers, the sergeant gave up and let her go. She left the room without a word or a backward glance, and she was well outside the door and around the corner before her knees turned to jelly and she had to lean against the wall.

She heard the sergeant quite clearly as he spoke to the patrolman.

"She knows something, Lefkowicz. Did you see, when I asked her that one question? Her eyes moved. Stupid, stubborn Swede, too dumb to know the safest thing is to talk to the police. I'll be back, you can bet your fine new boots, and I'll get it out of her. Now let's get out of here and up to where there's some air before I smother."

Hilda melted into the back stairwell.

The newspapers! Sir, they are the most villainous, licentious, abominable, infernal—Not that I ever read them!

—Richard Brinsley Sheridan,

The Critic, 1779

xcuse me, sir, but it's a bit of a walk back to the station, and —er—"

The door to the ground-floor lavatory stood slightly ajar. Patrolman Lefkowicz gestured, his face pink.

"Oh, for the love of Pete! All right, then, but be quick about it! I'll wait for you outside."

The sergeant headed out the back door. Hilda hesitated. Did she dare speak to the patrolman? He had seemed sympathetic, but . . . She hovered, indecisive and slightly embarrassed, until the patrolman came out of the lavatory, and then made up her mind and darted back into the hall.

"Excuse me. I am sorry to be a bother to you, but do you

mind—is it a trouble—will you take a message for me?"

She spoke in a near whisper, and young Lefkowicz replied in kind.

"I'm sorry, miss, but I must go."

"It is only to the firehouse," Hilda pleaded. "I wish to give Mr. Cavanaugh a message, but I cannot leave the house in the morning."

"The central firehouse?"

"Yes. It is not so far from the police station, *ja?*"

Hilda's golden hair was curling damply around her face. Her fair skin was flushed with the heat, and her uniform, also damp, clung to a figure that was as fine as any the patrolman had ever seen. He smiled nervously. "All right, but I have to hurry!"

"Just" (it came out *yoost* in her agitation, and she tried again), "just, please, ask Patrick to come to see me when he can. I will be outside, near five o'clock, every day."

"Lefkowicz!" A bellow came down the outside steps.

"Yes, sir!" He grinned at Hilda, winked, and hurried down the hall as she gazed after him.

"Hilda! What are you gaping at, girl?" Mr. Williams materialized out of the servants' room. "The family are down, and here you are lollygagging about! Upstairs with you! And put on a clean uniform and apron—you're a disgrace!"

Between the unrelenting heat, Mr. Williams's nagging, and her own uncomfortable thoughts, Hilda was in a thoroughly bad temper by mid-afternoon. There was usually an hour or so after lunch when she could rest, but when she tried to lie down on her bed, both her room and her brain felt so stuffy she could find no peace.

She sat up and knocked on the wall by her bed. "Norah! Are you awake?"

"Depends who's asking," replied a muffled, sulky voice.

"I come over," said Hilda decisively, and stepped into the narrow hall, looking both ways before scuttling to Norah's room in her petticoat.

Norah didn't look up as Hilda entered.

"I am sorry," she said, very formally, before her friend could utter a word. "I was not polite to you this morning, and I apologize. I had bad dreams last night, and slept only little, but I should not have said what I did. Will you forgive me?"

She stood, blue eyes fixed on Norah's, hands clasped primly in front of her.

Norah began to laugh. "Ah, and it's too hot to hold a grudge. And it's a sight ye look, me girl, with yer hair comin' down, and walkin' about in yer shift. Ye'd best not let Mr. Williams catch ye."

"I think," said Hilda, still primly, "it would be worse if John Bolton would catch me."

"Hark at ye! Looking pious and butter-won't-melt-in-me-mouth, and talkin' like that. I thought ye were a good girl."

"*Ja*, I am," said Hilda, "but that does not mean I am also stupid. My English may not be perfect, always, but I can understand the look in a man's eye as well as you." She removed Norah's apron from the room's only chair and sat down, resting her elbows on her knees and her chin in her hands. "Norah, what did the police ask you?"

Norah yawned mightily. "Nothing much. If I saw anything, heard anything. I don't think he cared a tinker's damn for what I answered. He thinks I'm just stupid Irish."

Hilda stood up again and began softly to beat one fist into the other palm. "But that is what he thinks of all of us! You are stupid Irishwoman, I am stupid Swede. And also, we are only servants. He is so—so—I cannot remember the word in English."

"Prejudiced?" suggested Norah with a wry smile. "Bigoted? Self-important?"

Hilda nodded vigorously. "*Ja—just det.* All of those things. He is so *ignorant*, Norah—that is the word! He will not try to find the truth, nor will the superintendent. They will decide, among them, on someone who did this terrible thing, and it will be someone like us, someone who does not matter, someone unimportant. It could be me, Norah, or you, so long as it causes them no trouble. That is all they care about!"

She was pacing by now in the small room, four steps to the window, four steps back.

Norah lay on her bed, unmoved. "And it's always been that way, me girl, and it always will be. Are ye just findin' out what this great land of America is really like?"

"But it is not *right!*" Hilda turned, her eyes ablaze. "It is *wrong* for an innocent person to be blamed—"

"And ye don't know that's what will happen," Norah interrupted. "Ye're lettin' yourself get all worked up, and all because ye didn't like the way ye were talked to. I'm sayin' ye'd best get used to it, and learn to take it, meeklike. Ye're a bright girl, Hilda, and ye've done well enough for yerself so far, but ye take things too much to heart. It's as yer friend I'm tellin' you, stop tryin' to change the world. It don't want to be changed."

Hilda bit her lip and sighed gustily. "But it should be changed. It needs to be changed."

"Well, if it ever is, it won't be by the likes of us, so calm yerself, and get a bit of a rest. We'll be on our feet soon enough."

Hilda would have stamped her foot if she hadn't remembered that she didn't want Norah angry at her again. Instead she shook her head decisively. "I cannot rest. I am too angry. I think I will take

all of the hearth rugs outside and give them a good beating. It is
what I would have liked to do to that sergeant this morning!"

"Suit yerself; I'm too hot. And it's going to storm." Norah
turned over with a creak of bedsprings. "Mind ye put yer frock
on, first!"

HILDA PUT ON the uniform she had discarded earlier at Mr.
Williams's command. It was still damp with perspiration. It was
wrinkled, and it smelled. But she would get hotter still beating
rugs, and she hadn't enough clean uniforms to change twice in
one day. She would be at the back of the house; it wouldn't matter
how she looked. Nevertheless, she retrieved the hearth rugs with
stealthy haste, lest the butler see her looking like that—or, worse
still, one of the family.

She didn't bother to take all twenty rugs. That would have
meant at least three trips in and out, with the attendant risks.
Besides, the rugs didn't in the least need beating. Hilda had
beaten the soot and ashes out quite thoroughly a couple of weeks
before, after what seemed likely to be the last fires of the season,
and the dust of summer hadn't yet settled in so that it couldn't
be removed with pan and brush.

No, she thought as she draped a rug over the clothesline
back by the carriage house and gave it a sturdy whack, she was
merely venting her frustration. And my, it felt good, even
though she panted with exertion in the heavy, stifling air. Take
that, Mr. High-and-Mighty Sergeant, she whispered in Swedish, and landed another blow that thudded like the strike of a
hammer.

Facing away from the house, she did not see them until they
were nearly upon her.

"Miss, I need to speak to you!"

"What can you tell us about the murder?"

"Was it you who found the body?"

"Who do you think committed this terrible crime?"

There were only two of them, but they sounded like twenty. Notebooks in hand, they ran from the front drive, shouting questions as they came.

"I'm a reporter for the South Bend *Tribune* . . ."

"I write for the South Bend *Times* . . ."

Hilda backed away, rug beater in hand. "*Nej, lägg av!*" she cried, her English deserting her in the crisis. *No, leave me alone!*

Far from discouraging the reporters, the remark inflamed them. "That's Swedish!" said the *Times* to the *Tribune* joyfully. "She *is* the one! Now look here, Miss Johnson—"

Hilda had a quick mind. It took her only a moment to get it in working order. "*Nej, jag kan inte engelska.*" *No, I do not speak English.* She advanced a little, rug beater still gripped firmly. The *Times* retreated a step or two, looking nervous, but the *Tribune* stood his ground.

"Miss Johnson, we know you speak English." He was speaking very slowly, and had raised his voice on the generally accepted principle that if English is spoken loudly enough, even an ignorant foreigner will understand. "You talked to the police yesterday. All we want to know is—"

"*Jag kan inte engelska,*" she repeated, fixing her face in the most vacant expression she could summon up. "*Jag måste jobba. Jag vill inte att Herr Williams skäller ut mig. Adjö.*" She walked around to the other side of the hanging rug and gave it such an almighty whack that it sailed off the clothesline, narrowly missing the *Times*.

He fled. The *Tribune*, made of sterner stuff, hesitated, but as

Hilda picked up the rug to rehang it, a lightning flash lit up the slate blue sky and an ominous thunderclap followed almost immediately.

A stupid Swede might not defeat him, but the wrath of God was too much. The *Tribune* pelted down the drive after his rival.

Hilda gathered up the rugs and made it to the basement just before the downpour.

Beware of giving servants the inch; there is no class so prone,
under such circumstances, to take the ell.

— Richard A. Wells,
A.M., *Manners Culture
and Dress*, 1891

The storm raged for the rest of the afternoon and evening,
fraying everyone's already strained nerves. Michelle darted
downstairs for brief intervals to pleat a collar or sponge a frill
in the laundry room, muttering words in French for which
nobody had the courage to ask a translation. Elsie lost her head
completely, had a fit of hysterics over the scullery sink, and went
to hide in a closet until the worst of the thunder was over, neither
the recriminations of Mrs. Sullivan nor the dire threats of Mr.
Williams having the slightest effect. Her dereliction of duty
meant that much more work for Hilda and Norah, and even
young Anton (who was nearly as frightened, but tried to hide it)

was pressed into service to help with washing greasy pots and pans after he'd finished serving dinner with Norah. Hilda, though she didn't really expect Patrick in a rain fit to float the Ark, had looked out of the east windows and the back door at five o'clock. He hadn't come, of course.

It was late when Norah and Hilda had finally completed their chores, and later still by the time they had washed the day's labors from their heavy black uniforms and hung them for the laundress to iron the next day. "Though how they're goin' to dry when the air's as wet as they are, I don't know," grumbled Norah, blotting her brow with a towel.

"At least it is cooler than it was," said Hilda with a sigh. "I will sleep, I think."

She slept soundly. Just as well, too, for it was in the morning that the real storm broke over her head.

She had awakened even before the usual time, to the riotous singing of birds. Though they had, by this late date in May, grown quieter than in the first frenzy of spring, the rain seemed to have aroused them again, and they were caroling so loudly that Hilda could not sleep. She lay for a few moments in peace, enjoying the music and the clear dawn. A fresh, gentle breeze blew in her west window. It was going to be a fine day.

As she dressed in her last clean uniform, she glanced over at the Harper house. All the blinds were down; the front door, she knew, would be shut tight, with a heavy veil of black crepe to discourage callers. It seemed a pity to close out the sun and air on such a day. She sighed for the sadness of the world and went downstairs.

She had barely reached the basement when her optimistic frame of mind was shattered.

"*Hilda!*" roared an awful voice from the servants' room.

Startled, she followed the voice. "Yes, Mr. Williams?"

He stood in the middle of the room, alone except for the faithful Rex. In his hand was the morning's edition of the South Bend *Times*. His face was purple and his hand shook as he pointed to the newspaper.

"What is the meaning of this?"

An awful apprehension stole over Hilda. She took the paper he thrust at her and read it, slowly and with growing horror. Fine print in English was still difficult for her, as was flowery journalese.

But the tenor of the story was all too clear. It purported to be an interview with "Hilda Johnson, ladies' maid at Tippecanoe Place" concerning the "horrible murder she was unfortunate enough to witness." It described her as "young and pretty, but terrified for her life" and hinted, without actually saying, that she thought one of the servants of the household was probably the killer, very likely the butler, "Mr. Williamson."

Dumbly, she handed the paper back to Mr. Williams. There was a dreadful silence while he waited for her to speak.

"Well?" he barked, finally.

"I—I cannot answer you. I do not know why they have written such things. I told them not'ing—"

"Do you mean to say you *talked* to reporters?"

"No, I—they come to me, I am outside, I clean the hearth rugs, I pretend not to speak English, I say not'ing at all—"

"Nothing, except to accuse me of murder!"

"*Nej*, Mr. Williams, I did not! I spoke no names—oh, *ja*, perhaps I said you would be angry with me for being slow with my work, but I said it in Swedish, and then the thunder came, and they were afraid, and they left, and I—"

" 'They,' " repeated the butler. "There was more than one?"

"Yes, one said he was from the *Times* and one from the *Tribune*."

"You spoke to two newspaper reporters—*newspaper reporters!*—against my express wishes to say nothing about this miserable incident, and you did not see fit to mention it to me!"

"But I did *not* speak to them! Even in Swedish, I say only things like, 'Go away,' and 'I do not speak English!' It is not my fault that they come to speak to me. I go to beat the hearth rugs—"

"And why, at this time of year? I gave no orders about the hearth rugs. You were waiting outside to meet that fireman friend of yours, of whom, I may say, I have never approved."

"I was not—"

"That will *do*, Hilda. I will not be answered back to by a chit of a girl. If we were not in sore need of your services, with reliable servants so hard to find, I should discharge you on the spot. As it is, you will go about your duties, and you will speak of this to no one. You will take your meals in the kitchen, and if I see you talking to Norah, or to any of the staff, about anything whatsoever, you *will* be discharged, servant shortage or no servant shortage. Do I make myself perfectly clear?"

She nodded, not trusting herself to speak.

"Then go and do your work, and see that you do it in exemplary fashion. I shall be keeping a very close eye upon you."

Rex, who had hidden under the footstool at the first sign of his master's anger, watched with mournful eyes as Hilda left the room.

She was very, very glad that the lavatory was just outside the servants' room, and that it was unoccupied. She closed the door behind her and leaned against its panels, taking deep breaths.

The tears that squeezed out from under her tightly closed eyelids were tears of anger and frustration. She was being made the victim of injustice and oppression, and there was nothing she could do about it. It was *not* her fault that someone had died. It was *not* her fault that police and reporters were dogging her heels. Yet she was threatened with the loss of her job. And in her subservient position, she could make no protest, raise no defense. She had no doubt that Mr. Williams would make good his threat to discharge her if she made any further trouble, and doubtless without a reference. Then it would be factory work for her, the Wilson Shirt Factory probably, if she could get work there, or if not—she shuddered at the thought. There were other ways a young, pretty girl could make money, but she was sure she would rather die.

It might yet come to that, if the police . . .

Stubbornness cuts both ways. This time it came to Hilda's aid and saved her from self-pity. She would *not* be beaten. She would *not* give in. She would do her work, as well as she had ever done it, or better, and give no one any reason to find fault with her. And if anyone dared accuse her of murder, she would prove them wrong if it took her last breath!

She bathed her reddened eyes in cold water, straightened her spine, and sailed out to tackle the day's duties after the manner of one killing tigers.

The butler had evidently conferred with the cook, for when Hilda went into the kitchen, as bidden, for her breakfast, Mrs. Sullivan had laid a small table for her in the corner, with an early rose nodding from a water glass.

"You don't want to pay too much heed to what he says, dearie," she whispered conspiratorially as she put Hilda's laden plate before her. "His bark is worse than his bite, y'know. Just watch your step for a few days."

Hilda flashed her a grateful smile, and found that she had to swallow a large lump in her throat before she could eat her bacon and eggs.

She kept herself furiously busy for the rest of the day and walked in the garden during her afternoon break, so as not to have to tell Norah she couldn't talk to her. But when she came in, Norah, a tray on one shoulder, was lying in wait for her.

"So there ye are. Not seen ye all day, have I, then? Well, ye can come in and help me set the dinner table and tell me why ye've not been to meals."

Norah gripped her wrist and led her firmly into the state dining room.

"Now." She set down her tray of napkins and cutlery. "There's somethin' wrong, and don't try to tell me different."

Hilda shook herself free, picked up a napkin, and began to fold it into the elaborate five-pointed shape preferred by Mrs. Clem for dinner parties. She shook her head.

"Hilda Johansson, don't clam up on me! I'm tryin' to help ye, my girl!"

"I am not allowed to speak to you," she muttered. "I am not allowed to speak to anyone. Please do not ask me, Norah. I could lose my position here." She pressed her lips together and tried to move away, but Norah caught her wrist again.

"It's that Mr. Williams, isn't it?" Norah persisted, but in a lower tone. "He told us at breakfast that ye weren't to be bothered, that ye were 'upset.' I could tell he wasn't telling the truth, not by half. And another thing, none o' the newspapers were around. John Bolton, he came in and wanted to read the *Times* this afternoon, and Mr. Williams told him he'd thrown it out. As if he ever did! It's Anton does the tidying up, and anyway, the papers are saved for making up fires, as ye well know." She was laying out cutlery on the gleaming damask tablecloth as she spoke.

She reached the end of the long table and turned the corner. "So if it's His Superiorness ye're worried about, he's polishing the big silver compotes in his pantry. He's just begun, and it'll take him a good, long time: Hilda, tell me quick!"

Hilda busied herself for another moment or two, then reached a decision.

"*Ja*. I will tell you. You will not talk about it."

It was more an order than a question, and Norah glared at her. "As if I would!"

"No, but I must make sure. Mr. Williams is angry because reporters from the newspapers came to talk to me yesterday, when I was outside. I told them nothing—I pretended I could speak no English—but they put something in the newspaper. It was all lies, all made up, but Mr. Williams did not believe me. So he has told me not to speak to anyone, about the murder or anything else."

"The stupid, arrogant son of—"

"*Ja*." Hilda's face was grim. "But he is in authority. I must be careful, Norah. I believe that he really would discharge me, and then . . ."

She left the rest unspoken, but Norah knew well enough what Hilda's options would be if she lost her job. She made a face and nodded. "So ye're going to drop it?"

Hilda frowned. "Drop? I do not drop things, I am careful, never have I broken—"

Norah laughed shortly. "Oh, Lord, yer English is so good, I forget sometimes ye don't know everything. I mean, ye're going to be sensible and stop meddling in things that are none of yer affair, like murder and bodies and the Lord knows what all?"

"Of course not!" Hilda finished with a napkin and set it in place with a smart thump that almost undid its careful folds. "I will be careful, that is all. I will be secretive and dis—dis—"

"Discreet?" suggested Norah, her tone of voice suggesting incredulity.

"Discreet, *ja*." Hilda ignored her friend's attitude. "And you will help me."

"Ye're out of yer mind, me girl! Me, mixed up in—"

Quick, light footsteps sounded on the parquet floor outside the dining room.

Both girls stopped talking and turned back to their work.

"Oh, Norah, good. There will be two extra guests for this evening, quite unexpectedly, I'm afraid. I've come to tell Mrs. Sullivan myself; I don't wish her to be upset. I'm glad I caught you in time. Lay two more places, will you, child?"

Mrs. Clem smiled charmingly; Norah dropped a curtsey, and Hilda turned to do the same, both of them presenting a countenance as bland as they could make it.

Unfortunately, neither face was made for deception. Mrs. Clem studied them, her eyes narrowing. "What is it, Hilda?" she asked sharply. "Is something the matter?"

"No, madam," replied Hilda with another curtsey. "Thank you, madam."

Mrs. Clem looked at them thoughtfully for a moment, while Hilda carefully pleated and re-pleated the napkin in her hand. Then she shrugged.

"Very well, then. I won't keep you from your work."

The mistress of the house passed into the family dining room, doubtless on her way to the butler's pantry to confer with Mr. Williams, and the two girls sighed with relief and continued their work in silence.

Hilda finished what she could do in the dining room and escaped to the kitchen. Mrs. Sullivan was in an uncertain temper, as she almost always was when there were guests for dinner, but at least she kept Hilda far too busy to talk to anyone. Hilda was in the back of the storeroom, looking for a jar of the home-preserved brandied peaches the cook wanted to use as a garnish, when a touch on her shoulder made her gasp. She whirled around, nearly dropping the gooseberry jam she held in her hand.

John Bolton took it from her and replaced it on the shelf.

"Now, now," he said softly. "Mustn't blot your copybook, must you? Cook wouldn't like a mess in her larder."

"What do you want?" asked Hilda, turning again to hunt for the peaches.

"Not what you think," answered John with a rich chuckle. "Not at the moment, at least. Your young man's outside asking for you. I told him you're confined to quarters, so to speak, but he insisted, so I said I'd try to winkle you out."

"Patrick? He came, then! Oh, but Mr. Williams—"

"He's busy in his pantry just now. If you go out through the kitchen, he'll not see you—but mind you're quick about it."

Hilda's hand closed on the jar of peaches, which had providentially appeared at the back of the shelf. She nodded gravely to John, squeezed past him, and went out into the kitchen, where she handed the jar to the cook.

"Please excuse me, Mrs. Sullivan," she said demurely to the cook. "I must—that is, I must go upstairs for a moment."

It was their accepted euphemism for dealing with a woman's private necessities, and the one request that was unarguable. Mrs. Sullivan grumbled under her breath, but nodded. Hilda walked boldly out of the door into the hall and turned as if to go up the service stairs, but instead headed straight out the back door and flew up the steps, praying that the cook was too busy to glance out the kitchen windows.

Patrick was waiting for her at the head of the stairs.

"Hilda, I—"

She put her finger to her lips and drew him around the corner, against the wall of Mr. Clem's office. There, nestled in the corner by the chimney, they were safe from observation, at least from inside the house.

"What's all the fuss, Hilda me love? Why are they treatin' you this way? That bold-eyed spalpeen of a coachman, he said—"

"Patrick, please!" She spoke in an urgent whisper. "There is no time to explain. It will mean my job if they see us here. But quickly, quickly—you have friends in the police. Can you learn for me what the police are thinking, what they are doing? They hate me, they hate all foreigners—I am worried, Patrick!"

Patrick might have been full of blarney, but he was no fool. He could see that Hilda was deadly serious, and adjusted his manner.

"All right, then, don't worry—though I'll tell you the truth, I was worried meself for a little time. The sergeant thinks you're lyin', do you know?"

Hilda lifted her chin and said nothing at all, but looked daggers at him.

Patrick shrugged. "Well, then, I didn't say *I* thought so. But whether you are or whether you're not, there's no need to be afraid, Hilda. I've talked to me friends, and the police don't suspect you, or any of the staff. They're lookin' for a Chinaman."

"A *Chinaman!* But—oh, because she had come to here from China?"

He nodded emphatically. "They think someone followed her, someone with a grudge. Or else someone who lives here and has family back there, and the trouble is spreading. There's Chinese right here in South Bend, you know."

He raised his eyebrows and Hilda nodded impatiently, with an anxious glance at the corner of the house.

"They run laundries," Patrick went on, "but who knows what else they're up to? So they could have done it, maybe to get even with something that happened back in China. But there's no telling what one of them Chinee might have done, or why—"

Hilda exploded. "Patrick Cavanaugh, you should be ashamed of yourself! You, of all people, an Irishman! You ought to know how the immigrants to this country are treated. They scorn us, they hound us—yoost because we work hard and are not ashamed of it. Now you believe that the murderer is an immigrant, for no more reason than that he is foreign, he is not like us—"

Her voice was rising higher and higher, and Patrick clapped a hand across her mouth.

"Hush!" he said urgently. "You're talkin' too loud—someone will hear. And you're talkin' daft, besides. It's sense to be lookin' for a Chinee. They're killin' missionaries left and right over there, so why not here, too. And I'll thank you not to be sayin' I'm stupid!"

Hilda pulled his hand from her mouth, furiously. "I did not say you were stupid! But I am not stupid either. I read the newspapers. I know that, when someone is killed, nearly always the killer knows the poor man, or woman. But the police will not look at Miss Harper's friends, or her family—oh, no! They are too important, too respectable—"

"Hilda Johansson, are ye daft? Sayin' it might be someone in Judge Harper's family? That's slander, girl, there are laws against—"

Somewhere a door opened. Patrick closed his mouth, and Hilda froze like a frightened rabbit as footsteps sounded on the basement stairs.

"Where are you going to, my pretty maid?" sounded John's light tenor, raised in song. "I'm off to the kitchen now, sir, she said . . ."

He changed to a whistle and sauntered down the path to the carriage house with never a glance their way.

Patrick scowled, but gestured to Hilda. "Cheeky! He means you'd best get in, Hilda, right now. I'll talk to you on Sunday, and mind ye keep your daft ideas to yourself, meantime!"

She got to the kitchen at least ten seconds before Mr. Williams did.

In the morning they are like grass which groweth up. In the morning it flourisheth, and groweth up; In the evening it is cut down, and withereth.

—Psalm 90, from the
"Service for the Burial
of the Dead,"
Methodist Episcopal Church

I should like to go, sir." Hilda stood before Mr. Williams, her head held high, her gaze unwavering. "My work is done, and the family will not need me. They will all be there. I will be silent, and not push myself forward, but I should like to go."

"It is a Saturday, and there are guests in the house. You are wanted here, and there is no need for you to go," said Mr. Williams.

"Sir, there is need, for me. You did not see her. I did. I have nightmares, sir. I should like to see her buried decently, like a Christian."

She was not going to plead. Her heart might be pounding with her apprehension of what he could do to her, but this was a reasonable request, and she was just as important a human being as he was, and her stubborn pride would not let her give way to his unreason.

"It's unsuitable."

"I should like to go, sir."

It took another ten minutes, but water will wear away stone eventually. After Hilda promised faithfully, and hypocritically, not to speak to a soul about any subject whatsoever, Mr. Williams capitulated with bad grace, and Hilda sped upstairs to prepare for Miss Harper's funeral.

There was some truth in her excuse. She continued to have nightmares, and once she had seen Miss Harper's body laid safely in the ground, she might be free of them. But it was only an excuse; her real reason was that she wanted to watch the Harper family. And if Mr. Williams had known *that*, she would have been locked up.

Maybe Patrick was right, and it was foolish to suspect any of the Harpers of the murder. What reason would they have to kill a harmless old-maid missionary? Certainly it was dangerous to air such thoughts. The rich and powerful had ways of squashing impertinence in the poor and humble; they did it as casually as they would squash a mosquito, and with nearly as little trouble.

Nevertheless . . .

Hilda owned but few clothes, and nothing really suitable for a funeral. A black uniform dress would have to do. With her winter hat, which was black, black gloves, and her apron left at home, she would (she hoped) be unrecognizable. People don't ever really look at servants, she had found.

The First Methodist Episcopal Church was in the center of town, as befitted a large and fashionable church. Hilda had only five short blocks to walk. She waited to set out until both the Harper and Studebaker carriages had left. It wouldn't matter if she were a little late; she intended, in any case, to sit at the back where she could see without being seen.

The carriages moved at a suitably funereal pace. There was a good deal of traffic on the streets of a Saturday afternoon, both wheeled and on foot, and Hilda, who had to walk slowly to avoid overtaking her employers and neighbors, blended in nicely. She got to the church just as the Harper families were dismounting from their carriages.

The judge, in black frock coat, wing collar, and top hat, looked much as he always did, but stooped and worried and far older than he had appeared to Hilda only a few weeks before at the dinner party when he had announced his candidacy for office. It was hard for Hilda to tell anything about Mrs. Harper's emotions, swathed as she was in black from head to toe, with a heavy black veil covering her face. Mr. James, Hilda was shocked to see, stumbled as he stepped out, and would have fallen but for the strong arm of the footman. Surely he hadn't been drinking before a funeral?

The married daughters and their husbands were in a second carriage, a smart landau. Again Hilda was disappointed. The men looked entirely conventional, if a bit tired, and the women's veils hid them from public view. Their mourning clothes, in Hilda's opinion, were overly ostentatious. Mrs. Reynolds's dress ran to frills that weren't especially becoming to her plump figure, and Mrs. Stone's clothing carried such a weight of jet beads that Hilda wondered how she could keep her shoulders back.

There was a subdued bustle as the party moved into the church, followed by the servants from all three households, who had ridden in a hired rig. Hilda moved back; she had no desire to be seen by Annie, who in any case was looking quite above herself. Hilda made a little noise of disgust. That Annie, giving herself airs just because she'd gotten to ride in a carriage! And at a funeral, too; she should behave in more seemly fashion.

The family members were escorted down the aisle by the minister, while the servants filed into their reserved pew at the back of the church. The few stragglers, Hilda among them, waited in sober silence to be escorted to their seats.

Inside, the organ was playing something subdued and mournful. Hilda was glad of the wait; it gave her a chance to get her bearings. In spite of herself, she was impressed and intimidated by the church. It was huge, far bigger than her tiny frame church. The organ had at least three times as many pipes, ranked in an imposing semicircle at the front of the sanctuary, as the new one the Swedish church was so proud of. As for the altar rail, its curve seemed to extend forever, and the pews, arranged in a curving pattern to match, would seat hundreds of people.

Indeed, they had to. The church was nearly full of decorous black, surmounted by black hats of huge and wonderful construction and the gray and balding heads of the men. The only seats left seemed to be in the back row, or at the far left end of the front pew. She had fully intended to sit in the back, but she hadn't anticipated such a crowd. She had come, after all, to see, and she would be able to see nothing over all those enormous hats. After a moment of indecision, she nodded to the usher, agreeing to the front seat and praying nobody would notice her. Especially not the Studebakers! Anyway, the seat was close to a side door, so she could leave if she had to.

She didn't stop to analyze the reasons for finding an escape route desirable.

Once seated, she looked discreetly at her lap for a few minutes before daring a quick glance around the church. Her choice of seats, as it turned out, had been fortunate. The entire Harper family was seated in the front pew to the right of the center aisle, facing the black-draped stand where the coffin would be placed. The curved seating arrangement let Hilda see them quite well. Not that there was much to see. The judge and his wife were sitting bolt upright, neither moving nor speaking to one another. Mr. James, slouched next to his mother, looked pasty and distinctly ill. Mrs. Stone sat next to her brother, with her sister beside her. The rest of the pew was empty. The two women were whispering to each other; Mrs. Reynolds took a black-bordered handkerchief out of her reticule and applied it to her eyes.

Hilda would have given a good deal to see under the veil and know if tears were really flowing down that petulant face.

Before she had a chance to spot the Studebaker family, the minister entered, the congregation stood, and the organ began a dirge as the coffin was borne in by six sturdy men, Mr. Reynolds and Mr. Stone among them. They took their seats next to their wives as the minister directed the congregation to remain standing for a hymn. Hilda found the words depressing and the unfamiliar tune hard to sing; she gave it up and watched the Harpers over the rim of her hymnbook.

The only Harpers making any attempt to sing were the daughters. Mrs. Stone's voice could be heard clearly, a little off-key. Mrs. Reynolds had a better voice, but it cracked halfway through the first verse and she once more applied her handkerchief to her eyes. Maybe she was really upset, then, thought Hilda with a touch of surprise.

The two sons-in-law, the first half of their duty accomplished, were plainly bored. They held their hymnbooks open, but scarcely glanced at them. Hilda couldn't remember which one was Mr. Stone and which Mr. Reynolds, since they looked

much alike—in their thirties, prosperous, clean-shaven, with
well-barbered dark hair. One of them fiddled with his cravat, the
other glanced around the church. His eye caught Hilda's; she
looked hastily down at her hymnbook.

They were seated, listening to a Bible reading, before she
dared another glance. The judge was beginning to look really
terrible, she thought. His face was much the same color as his
graying beard; his hands moved restlessly on his knees. Mrs. Harper's head turned toward him with a sharp movement; presumably she whispered something, for his hands settled and stilled.
Mrs. Harper's own black-gloved hands were clasped tightly in
her lap, but her thumbs toyed with the bottom of her veil and
Hilda was startled to see the fine material part under the pressure.

Funerals were never happy occasions, but Hilda had seldom
seen so much tension displayed. Was it simply because of the
circumstances of this death, or was there something more in the
air? Hilda sighed deeply, got a sharp look from the woman seated
next to her, and decided she'd better pay attention for a while.

They stood again for another unfamiliar hymn, and Hilda
saw Mrs. Harper prod her son sharply in the ribs. He got to his
feet belatedly. There was one member of the family who wasn't
jumpy, anyway. Was it because he was barely conscious?

The service in the packed, stuffy church dragged at last to
its end, and the congregation got to its feet out of respect for the
dead. The coffin was carried out. Now was the time for Hilda to
melt out of the building by the side door and get back to work,
but she hesitated. She'd learned nothing useful, and Mr. Williams
was already angry with her. She shrugged. Might as well be
hanged for a sheep as for a lamb. She hung back as the Harpers
walked slowly up the aisle and the rest of the mourners followed
before she slipped meekly out the side door and was nearly un-
done.

"Why, Hilda, I had no idea you planned to attend. We would gladly have brought you with us."

It was Mrs. Clem, standing ready to get into the waiting carriage. Hilda prayed fervently for a hole to open up in the sidewalk and swallow her, but as none did, she gulped, curtsied, and tried to reply.

"I—yes, madam, I am sorry, madam—I thought—"

"Quite natural you should wish to be here," Mrs. Clem said firmly. "I think you'd better ride with us to the cemetery. It's a long walk on a hot day, and you'll feel better once you've seen her buried, won't you?"

Hilda looked Mrs. Clem straight in the eyes, too startled by her employer's perceptiveness to be properly subservient.

"Yes, madam, I think I will."

"Then come along. If you won't mind riding up top with John? I'm afraid there's no room inside."

In a moment Hilda was perched on the high seat beside the coachman with no clear idea of how she got there. John winked wickedly at her, but made no attempt at conversation on the ride to the city cemetery.

If she had been a little more relaxed, she would have enjoyed that ride. Never in her life had she been driven in a fine carriage. She decided she preferred sitting on the high driver's seat, where she could see everything and catch a breath of air now and then, to being cooped up inside. She could not smile in a funeral procession, but she began to preen herself a little as passersby stopped, gentlemen's hats removed, ladies standing with heads bowed. All this deference, of course, was to the dead, not to her, but she could nevertheless enjoy it, discreetly. It never entered her mind that her behavior was exactly what she had disapproved of in Annie.

When they arrived at the cemetery, Hilda was in something of a quandary. Would Mrs. Clem expect her to stay with the

Studebaker family? John helped her down from her high perch with an entirely inappropriate pat or two, for which she would have slapped him under any other circumstances. As it was, she had to content herself with a fierce glare, which upset John not at all.

She helped Mrs. Clem out of the carriage and curtsied. Her employer smiled, but walked off with her husband without a backward glance. Hilda took it that she was free to stand wherever she chose, and made for a tree behind which she could be inconspicuous.

Not many of the mourners had bothered to come to the cemetery. It was hot, they had done their social duty, and they wanted to get home to their suppers. Thus it was that Hilda found herself standing close behind the Harper family, close enough to observe the only interesting exchange all day.

It happened when the judge lifted a shaky hand to remove his hat, as the graveside service was about to begin. His nervous fingers could not retain their hold on the shiny silk, and the hat rolled merrily along the ground, stopping just short of the edge of the gaping hole in the earth made ready to receive Miss Harper's casket. A muted gasp passed through the company of mourners.

"Pick it up, James, and hold it yourself," Mrs. Harper hissed to her son. "And you, William, get hold of yourself. No matter what you've done, there's no need to make a public spectacle of yourself!"

The judge looked at his wife, and Hilda saw a tear roll slowly down his cheek.

A reverential regard for religious observances, and religious
opinions, is a distinguishing trait of a refined mind.
—Richard A. Wells, A. M.,
*Manners Culture and
Dress*, 1891

unday morning. The entire population of Tippecanoe Place
—family, servants, and guests—were making ready to observe the Sabbath. Even Rex, the bull terrier, and Biddy, the
cat, were subdued, as befitted the solemn nature of the day—or
perhaps because there was far less commotion in the servants'
quarters than on a weekday. Mrs. Clem was adamant that the
servants' work be kept to a bare minimum on their day of rest, so
all meals were cold, and the tidying of bedrooms and bathrooms
comprised the housework.

Hilda, in the "Sunday best" clothes she had worn for her
afternoon with Patrick, was headed out the back door, prayer

book in hand, when Mr. Williams came up behind her.

"A moment, Hilda."

"Yes, sir," she replied, her heart in her mouth. Had he seen her riding in—or rather on—the carriage yesterday? He couldn't dismiss her for that, surely, since it was at the invitation of Mrs. Clem. Had he seen her talking to Patrick on Friday, and only now decided to confront her with it? The superstitious thought crossed her mind that perhaps he could read her thoughts, her terrible suspicions of the judge. She swallowed hard, trying to down her fears and look him in the eye.

"I cannot forbid you to attend church," he said, frowning portentously. "Indeed, I would scarcely wish to do so, since you sorely need its calming influence to quiet your overactive imagination. However, I will remind you that you are not to discuss the—er—tragedy with your family or anyone else."

"I will remember what you said, sir," Hilda said with careful ambiguity.

"You will further remember that the dignity of this house and this family is extremely important. On men like the Studebakers hang the very future of this country, of our democracy—"

"Yes, sir. Will you excuse me, sir? I will be late if I do not hurry."

"Just one more thing. Mrs. Studebaker has been speaking to me," he said, and Hilda swallowed again. Her gloved hands clutched her prayer book tightly. "Mrs. Clement Studebaker, that is to say. She seemed—er—most impressed by your attendance at the funeral. I wished you to know that she has a certain degree of sympathy with you, so that you will be careful not to betray her confidence."

"Thank you for telling me, sir. May I go?"

He dismissed her with a curt nod. She waited until she was well outside before releasing her breath in a gusty sigh.

She was not, in fact, in much danger of being late, but she had to get away from him before he forced her to make a promise. Promises had to be kept. Unreasonable demands, according to Hilda's somewhat flexible code, did not always have to be obeyed.

There was quite enough time to wander over to the edge of the lawn and look at the fine row of irises blooming at the foot of the low wall separating the Studebaker front lawn from that of the Harpers. Hilda stood and admired them, breathing in their heady scent and trying to compose her mind to Sunday thoughts. It was some little time before her ideas on the subject of Mr. Williams could be quelled.

As she turned to go, Annie, dressed in unrelieved black, came around the corner of the Harper house.

"Good morning, Annie," said Hilda in the subdued tones one used to a person in mourning. Though in Annie's case, she thought, the black was probably more a form required by her mistress than any expression of grief for poor Miss Harper. "I am sorry about Miss Harper. I have not been able to tell you, until now." She didn't particularly want to talk to Annie, but the civilities must be observed.

"Yes, well, the Lord giveth and the Lord taketh away."

The Lord, in Hilda's opinion, had had very little to do with this taking away, but she didn't argue the point. "You look very tired. It must have been hard for you."

"Hard enough," said Annie sourly. "And as if we didn't have enough trouble in the house, here's that Wanda gone off gallivanting somewheres!"

"Wanda?"

"You know, the new help. Only been here a couple months, since Bridget went and got herself married. You've met Wanda. She was here that night you played at being ladies' maid, all la-di-da you were."

Hilda ignored that. "Ah, I remember now," she replied. "A Pole, *ja?* And did she also go to get married?"

"Don't know. Don't care. Just went off without a word to nobody. Yesterday mornin', it was, she never come to work, and she never come to the funeral, neither. Mrs. Harper, she sent a messenger to her roomin' house, but she wasn't there. Just like a foreigner, is what I say."

Hilda had known Annie too long to take the slur personally. Annie, one of the few native-born Americans among the host of servants who worked in the neighborhood, resented the lowliness of her own position and at the same time looked down on the immigrants, but she had ceased to think of Hilda as a "foreigner," and regarded her simply as a fellow servant.

"And what did the messenger learn of her?"

"Nothin'. He asked ever'body that knew her, but they all claimed they didn't know nothin'. And the end of it is, I've got to do all the work myself, and I don't get my whole Sunday off! And here I am wastin' some of it talkin' to you!"

She turned on her heel. Hilda rolled her eyes and set off for church with several more uncharitable thoughts on her conscience. As she walked, she made plans.

The Swedish Lutheran Evangelical Church, situated close to the Studebaker and Oliver factories, was well over a mile away, and what with chatting to Annie, Hilda was very nearly late after all. Her elder sister, Gudrun, was waiting for her by the gate of the small clapboard building and led her inside with scant ceremony to join Freya and Sven just as the first hymn was struck up on the wonderful new organ.

Basking in the familiar atmosphere of sisterly bullying and her native tongue, Hilda settled herself to the comforts of worship.

She enjoyed going to church, on the whole. It was, of course, one's duty, and duty can be irksome, but it was the only occasion afforded her, all week long, to be thoroughly Swedish. The little church looked, inside and out, a great deal like the one in Björka where she and her siblings had been baptized. The service, of course, was identical. Pastor Forsberg was younger than the *prast* at their village church, but his beard looked much the same, and he preached the same sort of sermons. If Hilda didn't listen to every word, her thoughts tending to wander off to more immediately pressing matters, at least she found the rise and fall of the lilting Swedish very soothing.

Too soothing. Gudrun's sharp elbow in her ribs roused her, and she sat up straight and opened her eyes very wide. The day was warm. Flies buzzed in and out of the open windows, palm-leaf fans kept up a lazy rhythm. Hilda hadn't slept well for two nights. She sighed and tried to listen.

" 'Am I my brother's keeper?' The question takes on new meaning in this modern world, in this country of America, where one's brother under God may speak a different language, practice a different religion, have foreign ways very different from the ones we find dear and familiar. Are we then to be absolved of the responsibility to care for him, to lead him in the ways of the righteous, to protect him from his error and from the persecution others may inflict?" Oh, dear. That was uncomfortably relevant. Sermons had no business touching one's real life that way. Church ought to be a time to relax in the satisfaction that one was doing good.

She was relieved when the sermon was over and she could apply herself to prayers, which gave one a good excuse to let one's head drop low and close one's eyes. Thank goodness this was not one of the Sundays when Holy Communion lengthened the service by a good half hour.

Fortunately, the closing hymn was loud and stirring. Once

on her feet, Hilda was wide awake enough. She sang lustily, for the sheer joy of making noise after a week of tiptoeing and being circumspect around everyone. Gudrun started to shake her head at her, to reprove her for making too much noise, but Hilda smiled at her and was pleased to see reproof change to an answering smile. Gudrun was a good sister. Most of the time. So long as she lived in a different house.

They filed out of the church, shook the hands of Pastor Forsberg and his wife, and then gathered on the grass to talk. Though Hilda was proud of her facility with English, she loved this chance to speak Swedish with her family and friends. This morning, however, things did not begin well.

"And what is this, my little chick, about a body and a butler?" said Sven teasingly.

Hilda put her prayer book in her pocket and frowned. "How did you—oh, the newspapers."

"*Ja*, the newspapers, and it is no joke, Sven," said Gudrun severely. "Our Hilda being mixed up with murder, and knowing the murderer, as well!"

"We are lucky she was not murdered in her bed," put in Freya with a shudder.

It was time to put a stop to this, once and for all. She had to listen to it from Mr. Williams; from her family, she did not.

"Listen, all of you!" she said, so loudly that some of the other families turned around to look. She lowered her voice, but not her intensity. "Almost nothing that they printed in the newspaper was the truth. I did not know that they were allowed to lie, but they did. I did find a dead woman, a murdered woman, and she was really the sister to the judge at the house next door to the Studebakers. Everything else is made up. No one in our house had anything to do with it."

"But you said—" began Gudrun.

"I said nothing at all to the reporters, except in Swedish. I had to pretend I did not speak English so that they would leave me alone. I knew I would get into great trouble if I spoke to them—and I did, even though I did nothing wrong!"

Gudrun might berate her sister, but she was fiercely loyal. She switched instantly from attack to defense, reached out an arm, and pulled Hilda to her protectively. "You are in trouble, my little one?"

"*Ja.* Mr. Williams was very angry with me for what they said I said." She decided not to tell her family that she had been threatened with the loss of her job. It would worry them too much, and Gudrun might very well join her voice with Mr. Williams's. "He told me I might not speak with anyone about the crime, and even forbade me to speak to the other servants at all."

"Even Norah?" asked Freya, who knew what a good friend Norah was.

"Especially Norah."

"You are talking to us," Freya pointed out.

"I did not promise." Hilda tossed her head. "He asked if I understood what he had said, and I said yes. But I made no promises. Mrs. Clem, she is on my side, I think, so I am not worried. And I will talk to my family about what I choose! So long as I am careful, I am not worried."

"But, Hilda!" said Gudrun, her face grim. "How can you not worry? There is a woman, dead, and no one knows who her murderer is. None of us can rest easy until this killer is in the hands of the law! What are the police doing to find him?"

This was going to be the sticky part. Hilda took a deep breath. "They are doing something that I think is very foolish and very wrong, Gudrun. They do not like foreigners, you know, and I think they are going to arrest someone Chinese, maybe not because he did anything wrong, but just because he is Chinese.

You heard what Pastor Forsberg said." How fortunate that she had actually listened for a little while. Now she must be very careful about what to say next.

"I think, me, that probably someone who knew Miss Harper was the one who killed her. That is why I cannot go home with you for dinner this afternoon. I must go to the police station and try to convince them of their mistake."

Battle was joined. It was conducted in subdued tones, out of respect for the other churchgoers around them and the proximity of the church, but it was nonetheless fierce. Gudrun was furious. Never mind that Sunday dinner at the tiny house the other Johanssons shared was a tradition as immutable as the law of the Medes and the Persians. If Hilda did not choose to partake of a family meal, a good Swedish meal such as she could not get all week long, and for which Gudrun and Freya had slaved since dawn, that was her affair. Furthermore, Hilda was out of her mind to think that Miss Harper could have been killed by one of her highly respected associates, and no matter what, Gudrun was not going to allow her youngest sister to have dealings with the police. Firemen were bad enough. She had never approved of Hilda's friendship with Patrick, not only a fireman but a papist, and look what it had led to. And as for dealing with *Chinese*, may the merciful Lord save us! Why Hilda couldn't find a nice Swedish boy to walk out with, she, Gudrun, couldn't imagine. Look at young Olaf Lindahl, respectable, well-to-do, and anyone with eyes in her head could see he worshiped the ground Hilda walked on . . .

Hilda, avoiding the touchier questions and ignoring side issues like the undoubted fact that Olaf Lindahl was fat and boring, argued from both sides at once. Patrick had nothing to do with it at all, she would have found the body without him, but he had everything to do with it, in that he had friends in the police and could supply her with information, and surely a Catholic was not really a heretic, whatever an old-fashioned Lutheran might think, and she, Hilda, was as entitled to her opinions as anyone else . . .

Freya followed the argument eagerly, agreeing now with one, now with the other. It was Sven who finally put an end to it.

"Sisters," he said, so quietly that everyone else had to stop talking to hear him. "This is an unseemly place for a quarrel, and Sunday is an unseemly day. Hilda, I believe that you have strong feelings about what you think you should do. I do not entirely agree with you, nor does Gudrun—obviously. But our Lord meant us to follow our conscience, as Pastor Forsberg reminded us this morning. Go, and do what you must, and may He be with you."

Hilda bowed her head to the blessing of her brother and went, feeling unusually sober.

A lady walks quietly through the streets, seeing and hearing
nothing that she ought not to see and hear . . .
> —Richard, A. Wells, A.M.,
> *Manners Culture and*
> *Dress*, 1891

I t had seemed a fine idea when she had thought it out, walking
to church that morning. It had still seemed wise in her
musings during the sermon, and the argument with her
family had, of course, stiffened her stubborn resolve.

Now that she was actually at the door of the police station,
matters seemed very different. She was about to deliver herself
into the hands of those who hated foreigners, those who
thought she was lying—as indeed she had been—or at any rate
had not been telling the whole truth. Could she keep up her
guard? Could she gain information without giving any, and
most especially without mentioning her fears about the judge?

Would it be better to go home and think further about her course of action?

"Can I help you, miss?"

A patrolman, coming out of the door, robbed her of her chance to flee. She took a deep breath.

"Yes, please. I wish to speak to—" Oh, *Herre Gud*, to whom? Patrick had mentioned the name of one of his friends, hadn't he? Now who— "To Patrolman Kline, please," she finished, praying it was the right name.

"Yes, miss, only he's not on duty today. Would you be a friend of his?"

"No. I do not know him. He is the friend of my friend. You may know him—Mr. Cavanaugh of the fire department."

"Ah, you're the beautiful Swedish girl he's always talking about!"

She drew herself up. Would she never be rid of the accent that gave her away? And what right had Patrick to be talking about her? They were friends, nothing more. Warm temper restored her resolve.

"I come here," she said with great dignity and as good an American accent as she could command, "on a matter of business. Would Patrolman"—she racked her memory for the difficult name—"Patrolman Lef—Lefke—"

"Lefkowicz, miss," replied the young policeman, jolted back into a formal manner by her hauteur. "Yes, he's here. Just ask at the desk, inside. Excuse me, miss."

He touched the bill of his small round hat and hurried off, and Hilda, taking a deep breath, opened the screen door and went inside.

The police station, a small frame structure with adjoining barn, was not an imposing building, but its atmosphere intimidated Hilda. There was a coldness here, a gray lack of humor or humanity. True to her nature, however, she squared her shoulders, raised her chin, and swept up to the desk in her grandest manner, twitching her skirts away from the several spittoons lining the walls. "Patrolman Lefkowicz, please," she said haughtily, careful to keep her voice level and monotone, like good, boring, unmusical American speech. "Tell him it concerns the Tippecanoe Place murder."

The patrolman leapt to his feet. "You know something about the murder, ma'am? You should speak to Sergeant Haney—he's out, but he'll be back soon—you shouldn't have come here, ma'am, it's no place for a lady. I can send him to you—"

"I have no time to wait." Panic at the name of the sergeant hoarsened her voice. She cleared her throat before continuing. "I wish to speak to Patrolman Lefkowicz."

"Yes, ma'am. He's in the barn, ma'am. I'll get him for you. If you'd like to sit down for a minute—" He looked around the room doubtfully, then took out his handkerchief and dusted off his own chair.

"Thank you. I shall stand."

It was working! She thanked all the gods at once, the old Norse ones as well, just to be on the safe side. He thought she was a lady. Now if she could just talk to the friendly patrolman before the dreaded sergeant returned . . .

The patrolman came on the run, bringing with him a smell of stables. Straw clung to his boots.

"Why, it's you! I thought—I mean, Alex said—I mean, Patrolman Bodkins—"

She put a hurried finger to her lips. "Perhaps, Mr. Lefkowicz, we could talk outside? Patrolman Bodkins said this is not a place for a lady."

She put a slight emphasis on the last word and fixed him with a meaningful stare. Thank heavens he was not stupid! Without a word he opened the door for her and ushered her out into the sunshine.

"You didn't tell them who you were," he said when they were safely out of earshot, around the corner.

"No. Tell me, Mr. Lefkowicz," she said, suddenly diverted by his fresh, pink, earnest face. "How can someone so intelligent as you work for that superintendent, when he is so—so scornful of foreigners? I could not keep my temper, I think."

"Well, Miss Johansson—is that the right way to say your name?"

"Yes," she said in some surprise.

"Mine's Lef-*ko*-vich."

"Oh. I am sorry, I—"

"It's all right. '*Lef*-ko-witz' is the way they all say it here, but I thought you and I, as immigrants together, should try to get it right. Would you like to sit on this bench?

"You see, miss," he went on when they were seated, "there are not so many good jobs for us Poles, not if we don't want to work in the factories. For the Irish neither. They think we're not reliable, and we drink too much."

"That is true, sometimes, with the Irish," Hilda said primly, smoothing her skirts.

"It is, and with us, too—sometimes," Lefkowicz admitted. "But most of us work hard. That's why we came to this country, to work hard and get ahead. There are a lot of immigrants in the police, you know, even a Swede or two."

Hilda knew, and she was profoundly grateful that they weren't around today, for they would have recognized her immediately and given her away.

"So, you see, there are more of us than of him—the super— and he's only here temporary, anyway. None of us think he'll stay long. More of a politician than a real policeman, if you take my meaning."

"I do understand you, and it is as I feared, Mr. Lefkowicz.

He wishes to make an arrest in this case quickly, *ja?*"

The patrolman nodded. "The quicker the better, as far as he's concerned."

"And he will not care if he arrests the right person or the wrong one, just so long as it is someone of no importance?" She had pronounced the *j* properly, the hard, ugly, American way, and was pleased with herself.

Lefkowicz hesitated, unwilling to commit himself so far. "There is good reason to suppose it is a Chinese man, Miss Johansson."

"*A* Chinese man?" Hilda pounced on it. "Have they learned something—I do not know the word—something to use against some particular person?"

" 'Evidence' is the word you want, Miss Johansson. Yes, they've found evidence enough. They've talked—that is, we've talked—to everyone in the two Chinese families that live here. If what they say is true, they haven't kept up contacts with China. They're even Christian converts, all of them, and good, steady churchgoers. Not much liked—well, you couldn't expect that— but quiet, respectable enough people, according to their neighbors. Besides, they work so hard in their laundries that they wouldn't have had a chance to go and murder somebody in the middle of the day, and the children were all in school."

"So . . . ," Hilda prompted.

"So, they did tell us that there is one Chinese man visiting in town. He is a Catholic convert, from a place with some very difficult name—I cannot say it. Anyway, his name—the Chinaman's—is Kee Long, which is easy, even if strange. He is visiting some of the fathers at Notre Dame, and we think—that is, the super thinks—that he might really be a spy from the Boxers in China, come to kill missionaries here."

Hilda felt a coldness creeping over her despite the hot sun.

"And where is your superintendent now?" she asked, afraid of the answer.

"He and the sergeant went out to Notre Dame in the patrol wagon to find this Kee Long fellow and talk to him."

"To hound him," said Hilda passionately, "to hunt him down, as the dog hunts the fox, to frighten him and confuse him until he admits to somet'ing—"

"Now, Miss Johansson," said Lefkowicz firmly, "calm yourself. There is no reason for you to have so little faith in the police, miss! We must question the man, of course. And if we think there is reason to believe he is guilty, he will be taken into custody. But there is a system of justice in this country. He will have a trial, he will go before a judge—"

Hilda stood and raised her hands to the sky, muttering something impassioned in Swedish before she turned to the hapless patrolman. "May *Herre Gud* have mercy on all fools! A *judge*, you say! And that judge will be the murdered woman's brother, or one of his friends! How much justice do you think Mr. Kee Long will find in *that* court?"

She was off, striding up Main Street before Lefkowicz could shut his mouth, much less reply.

She walked a block north, paying no attention, in her fury, to the businesses she was passing. They were all closed, of course; it was Sunday. The passersby, and there were many, were Sunday strollers like herself, walking off their dinners or taking a little turn to work up an appetite until the big meal should be ready. Carriages passed, many of them Studebaker carriages, from humble buggies to elegant landaus. They were filled with beautifully dressed couples coming home from church or going to luncheon at the Oliver Hotel. Hilda was very glad none of those terrible horseless carriages was on the street. There were one or two in town, but the noise they made, and the smell! Hilda preferred the honest smell of horses, though it could be strong when the sun shone as hot as it did today.

She had turned the corner onto Water Street before she realized that an idea had formed itself in her mind, and when it presented itself, insistently, to her consciousness, it took her breath away.

She was going to Notre Dame.

She sat down on a convenient bench to try to talk herself out of it.

Notre Dame was far away, out in the country. She didn't know how far; she wasn't even sure of the way. She did know that the only way to get there, if one had no carriage, was on foot.

Notre Dame was a stronghold of those strange and threatening people, the Catholics. And not only Catholics, but priests, and nuns, and brothers. It was one thing to have friends among the population of the ordinary Catholic laity. Even that made her uneasy sometimes, when Norah or Patrick would make the sign of the cross, or jingle strange beads in their hands, or say something peculiar about one of the saints, almost as if they knew them personally. But deliberately to walk into a nest of the most fervent papists! They would try to convert her to their idolatrous ways. Or they would take her prisoner and lock her up in a convent until her bones bleached. She had heard of such things.

Even if she escaped a terrible fate, it would certainly take her most of the afternoon to walk out there and back, and she was hungry. A good dinner was waiting for her at her family's house; she had only to walk in to be forgiven for her strange ideas and greeted with open arms and a loaded plate. Patrick, too, would be waiting for her, in the mid-afternoon. They nearly always walked out on Sunday if the weather was good. He would be disappointed if she were not there.

And at Notre Dame, home of the terrifying priests, a poor

hapless foreigner named Kee Long was being taken prisoner by the police.

She stood, brushed the wrinkles out of her skirt, settled her hat more firmly on her head, and began to walk, trying to think what Patrick and Norah had told her about the location of the university.

It was north, she knew, north and east. Well, in order to get very far east she had to cross the river, and there was a bridge on Water Street. After that—well, after that, she could ask somebody.

The closer she got to the river, the quieter the streets became, deserted on a Sunday. For this was South Bend's manufacturing district, or one of them. Of course the biggest factory in town, Studebaker Brothers, owned by her employer and his brother J.M., was in another section entirely, close to South Bend's other industrial giant, Oliver Chilled Plow. Neither of these plants was dependent upon water power; they used steam, and even electricity. But it was the river that had made South Bend what it was, and the river was still the heart of the town. The dam that spanned it, just downstream from the fine new Jefferson Street Bridge, harnessed its formidable power, and that power was used to the fullest. The scene was not beautiful, perhaps. Industry creates smoke and mess, and factories are seldom attractive, but Hilda thought it exciting. All that smoke from the never cool furnaces, all that work to begin again on Monday morning, all that money to be made, all that modern machinery ready to grind into action!

South Bend, in this year of Our Lord 1900, was a boomtown and no mistake. Lumber and feed were milled there along the river; paper was made, and woolen cloth, and Singer sewing machines, and plows—lesser plows, perhaps, than those with the proud Oliver name, but there was enough farmland to be tilled in the world to support more than one company. There was a small wagon manufactory, too, but Hilda gave it barely a thought. She might be gracious about plows, but Studebaker wagons were famous all over the world; Hilda turned up her nose at lesser firms. Her eye did linger for a moment on the factory and salesroom of Collmer Brothers Bicycles. One day, perhaps . . .

These were pleasant thoughts, enough to occupy her for a few minutes, but once the river was well behind her and she had passed (quickly) St. Joseph's Catholic Church, she entered a neighborhood of small, undistinguished homes. With little of interest to see, she was forced to think once more about what she was doing. Had she walked too far east? How much farther did she have to go?

A couple sitting on their front porch fanning themselves gave her the chance to ask.

"Excuse me," she called from the dusty path. The cedar block paving and the wooden walkway had ended some way back; now all was dirt, packed hard by the feet of horses and humans and the wheels of carriages. "Do you know the way to Notre Dame?"

"Open the gate, child, and come in," called the woman, a stout, pleasant-faced person clad in a pleated black Sunday costume that looked as hot as a blanket. "I'm hard of hearing."

Hilda did as she was bidden. "I walk to the University of Notre Dame, and I do not know if I am on the right road," she repeated when she had reached the porch steps.

"Well, now, I'm not just so sure," said the woman thoughtfully. "Do you know, my dear?"

Her husband, seated beside her, had decided that on his own front porch he could unbend from Sunday formality enough to take his coat off, and his vest, but he had kept his collar on, and his tie. He wrapped his thumbs around his suspenders and considered. "There's a street up there a block or two," he said, pointing vaguely east, "that calls itself Notre Dame. Heathen kind of a name, to my way of thinking, but it might take you there. Stands to reason, don't it?" He grinned at her. "You can't miss it. There's a school on the corner, Coquillard School."

"Thank you, very much." She smiled and turned to go.

"Stop a minute, child," said the woman, "and let me fix you some lemonade. You look powerful hot and tired, and I've heard tell that place is way out in the country."

Her whole soul cried out for cool, tart lemonade, but she shook her head. "I must go. If it is a long way, I do not have time to stop."

"Then take some with you. You can leave the glass when you come back. You look honest. Just you wait there for one minute."

The woman heaved herself out of her rocking chair and waddled into the house, to return only moments later with a large glass. It was filled with pale yellow liquid and a chunk or two of ice.

"And I brought you some gingerbread to go with it." She handed her a large heavy brown slab. "It'll go in your pocket."

"Thank you!" said Hilda from the bottom of her heart. "You are very good to a stranger."

"Well, dearie, that's what life is about, isn't it?" The woman smiled comfortably. Her hair fell in limp strings, and she smelled of stale talcum powder and of clothing washed too seldom. To Hilda she seemed an angel straight from heaven.

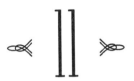

While students of all religious denominations are received into the University, it is nevertheless a strictly Catholic institution, and all students are required to attend divine service in the College Church at stated times.

—catalogue of the
University of
Notre Dame, 1900

efreshed by lemonade and gingerbread, Hilda made good progress down the dusty road. She nursed her drink for a long time, breaking off chips of ice to eat, as she had as a child, but finally it was gone, everything was gone, and she put the glass in the capacious pocket of her petticoat to return on her way back.

She had found Notre Dame Street with no trouble, only a block or two away, and turned left, passing Coquillard School and St. Joseph's Hospital. The hospital was only a small church, refitted for its changed duties, but Hilda quickened her pace as she passed it. She didn't care much for hospitals of any description; in a hospital run by nuns, anything might happen. This was a very *Catholic* part of town, Hilda thought with some trepidation. St. Joseph's Church, St. Joseph's Hospital, Notre Dame Street, Coquillard School—Alexis Coquillard, Hilda remembered someone having told her, was the man who'd founded South Bend some seventy or eighty years ago, and he was French, so certainly a Catholic!

Just a block or two past the hospital, at Sorin Street, Notre Dame Street seemed to come to an end. She could see nothing but trees and widely scattered houses. No magnificent building with a solid-gold dome. And no one in sight to ask.

If there had been a bench to sit on, Hilda might very well have sat down and cried. She was hot, she was tired, she was hungry and thirsty again, and it looked as though she had been going the wrong way. It wasn't fair! Notre Dame Street ought to lead to Notre Dame! As there was no place to sit, however, except in the rutted dust of the road or the grass off to the side, either of which would be ruinous to her clothing, she had no choice but to go on walking.

She walked, tentatively, a few paces into the middle of Sorin Street, and looked to the left and right. In both directions, she could see streets continuing north from Sorin. She looked from one to the other. Finally, with a sigh, she chose the one to the right; it was closer and there seemed to be more houses on it. If she couldn't find someone to ask, she would go straight up to a door and knock. Yes, she would. And even if a priest or a nun answered, she would stand her ground. They couldn't eat her, and she wasn't going to give up now that she had come this far.

She was not put to the test. As she turned into the street and looked anxiously down its length, there it was. A dome, gleaming so brightly gold in the sunlight that for a moment she thought it must be the sun, lost in the sky and wandering far to the north.

Well! She had found it!

So to speak. It looked a long ways away. Hilda sighed, wiggled one foot to try to dislodge the small stone that had settled near her heel, and, failing, plodded on.

The houses, spaced more thinly as she went, finally gave way to fields. Farmland to her right baked in the heat, young green spikes of corn rising in the neat hills of one field, wheat in another, oats in another. In the distance, though she could not see them, she could hear and smell pigs. It was very flat country compared to her homeland, with only a small rise or two to interrupt the monotonously level horizon—no beautiful mountains. Nevertheless, there was a familiarity to the scene that brought unexpected tears to Hilda's eyes. All farms, all over the world, must be very much alike.

What was her mother doing now, and her young brothers? A Sunday afternoon—no, Sunday evening it would be now, there. And the weather would be different. Somehow that thought, that she couldn't even visualize where the sun lay in the sky at home, or whether it was shining, made Hilda feel more alone, more lost, than she had felt since she'd left home. She didn't belong there anymore, had no part in the farm in Sweden that had been her home from birth. But neither did she belong here. A stranger in a strange land . . .

She shivered. The sun had surely passed behind a cloud; it was dark on the road. And she looked around her, seeing her real surroundings instead of the Swedish farm, and saw crosses and headstones and one large monument, and was engulfed by a wave of terror.

She began to run, heedless of the stone in her shoe. She didn't slow until she had put the cemetery well behind her and was surrounded once more by the trees on either side of the road. She stopped, then, and made herself look back to make sure nothing was following her.

It was a very small cemetery. Nothing to fear. Nothing at all. She was a fool.

But her panicky rush had carried her to the very portals of the Notre Dame grounds, and as she assessed her surroundings she was assailed by new worries. It was so big!

She had thought there would be one large building, like a school. Oh, very big, indeed, and very fine, but her imagination had not been capable of conjuring up anything like this! All around her stood buildings, yellow brick buildings of two or three or even more stories. The one just ahead of her, the one with the dome, was immense, one of the biggest places she had ever seen, with a confusing jumble of wings and stairs and doors and, on the very top, an immense golden statue, and of the Virgin Mary, surely! She had thought Patrick was making it up. She knew that Catholics had statues of the Virgin in their churches, and she had heard that they sometimes prayed to them, a practice of which she heartily disapproved. But to have one as big as this, and of gold! And right out there where no one could miss seeing it!

She very nearly turned around then and went back home. If she hadn't been so hot and thirsty she would have, but she needed a drink of water. Would people who would put up a statue like that have a drink of water for a Lutheran?

She wasn't sure. Not only that, but she had no idea whom to ask. There were people walking around the grounds, but they were all men, young men in suits, laughing and talking, who must be students, and older men in cassocks who must be priests. She could not approach an unknown man and speak to him.

If she had thought about it at all, she had thought she would simply walk in and ask someone on duty to speak to the priest who was entertaining the Chinese man. But that was before she realized how big this place was. Now she stood, irresolute. Surely that big building with the dome was the principal one. Was that where a visitor should go? Or were visitors, at least women visitors, perhaps not allowed? It was a men's college, she knew, but she thought there was also a convent here—frightening place that it was—

There was certainly a convent. Two nuns approached across the lawn, talking quietly together, their pleated white headdresses looking like oversized halos, their beads hanging at their sides. Hilda stared in awe, and then lowered her eyes. Staring was rude, even staring at so unlikely a vision.

But they were coming toward her! They were going to scold her for staring at them. No, they were going to try to drag her into the convent! She stood rooted to the spot, too terrified even to run.

"You look lost, child," said a practical sort of voice that reminded her of the friendly woman on the porch. "Are you visiting someone? Can we help you at all?"

She swallowed. "I—I do not know. I have never been here before, and I—" Her voice cracked, and she made a decision. Nuns, convents, idols, whatever terrors awaited, she must have a drink. She took a deep breath.

"Is there a place where I could yoost have some water?"

"Of course," said the other nun, a younger one, Hilda thought from her voice, though her wimple made it hard to tell. "You look awfully hot and dusty. Come with us; we were just going back home."

Home. The convent. "Oh—I do not know—"

"My dear girl," said the older woman crisply, "whatever you have heard, we do not eat Protestants. We don't even abduct them. And unless you sit down soon, you're going to faint; you're as white as your dress. There's a visitors' parlor, you know. No one will lock you up, I promise," she added dryly.

So it was that Hilda found herself sitting in a bare little room with a few chairs, a crucifix on the wall, and a small table in front of her with a pitcher of water, a glass, and some bread-and-butter sandwiches.

The older of the two nuns who had brought her there sat in the room with Hilda, and when she had quenched her thirst, the nun nodded sharply at the sandwiches.

"For you've eaten too little today, I believe. You have a pinched look about you."

"I had some gingerbread," said Hilda in a small voice.

The nun snorted. "Gingerbread! Much good that will do you! Did you walk all the way from town?"

"Yes." She took a bite of the bread and butter. It did taste good. She took another.

"Look here, child, you can tell me it's none of my business, and you'll be right. But something important brought you all the way out here on such a hot day, when you're scared to death of the place. You're Swedish, aren't you?"

Hilda nodded, her mouth full.

"And it isn't Pastor Forsberg who put all the nonsense about Catholics in your head, I'll be bound. He's a good, sensible man, though he goes his way and we go ours."

"You know Pastor Forsberg?" Hilda asked, incredulous.

"We've met, at community meetings and hospital visits. A good man," she repeated. "Now, do you feel up to telling me why you came here, so I can point you in the right direction?"

Hilda hung her head. "You are kind. I am ashamed. I have Catholic friends, I should have known, but—"

"It doesn't matter." The nun waited, her hands folded into her wide black sleeves.

Hilda gathered together the shreds of her dignity and spoke the simple truth. "I came to speak to the Chinese visitor, to Mr. Kee Long. I was told that he was the guest of a priest here. Or if the police—that is, if he is not here, I wish to speak to the priest."

Whatever the nun had expected, it was clearly not this. She looked at Hilda with shrewd eyes for a long moment.

"What is your name, child?" she asked finally.

"Hilda Johansson."

"Ah." There was a wealth of comprehension in her voice. "I am Sister Mary Elizabeth, and I begin to understand. You are involved in this terrible murder, aren't you?"

"I am not involved," said Hilda firmly. "I found her, that is all. I am concerned."

The nun's lips twitched a little. "You speak very excellent English," she said. "It's a fine distinction you've made there. And what is your interest in Mr. Kee Long?"

Hilda hesitated. "You will think I am foolish. Everyone thinks I am foolish."

"Most people are," said Sister Mary Elizabeth serenely.

"Well, then. I am a foreigner, and I know how foreigners are sometimes treated in America."

"A sin and a scandal," said the nun promptly. "We bring immigrants here to do our work, and then treat them like the dirt beneath our feet."

"Oh! You *do* understand! Then you will understand why I am afraid for Mr. Kee Long. The police think he killed the woman, but they have no proof. They think so only because he is Chinese. I believe that she was killed by"— she bit back the words in time—"by someone else, I do not know who, but I fear they will take him and be satisfied, because he is a foreigner."

Her manner was less passionate than usual, for she sensed

that in this woman she faced someone whom she did not have to convince.

Sister Mary Elizabeth nodded slowly. "We have been of your opinion, my dear. That is, those of us who have met the gentleman. Mr. Kee—the surname comes first in Chinese names, you know—Mr. Kee is a fine man and a sincere Christian. He came to America to escape persecution, not to inflict it."

"Then—then somehow he must understand his danger! The police are coming here to arrest him. I thought they would be here already. He must be hidden, or taken away, or—"

"My dear." The nun's eyes were full of compassion. "The police have been here. We could not refuse to cooperate with them, you must understand that. We told them, of course, that Mr. Kee could not have committed the murder, since he was here all that day. We might even have tried to insist that he be allowed to remain in our custody while his bona fides were established."

"But you must not allow them—" Hilda's temper was up, finally, and Sister Mary Elizabeth put her finger to her lips.

"Hush, child. Your English is perhaps not quite as good as I had supposed. I said that we 'might have' done this—had we been given the opportunity. Unfortunately, we were not. By the time the police arrived to talk to Mr. Kee, he was no longer here."

Hilda's brows drew together in a puzzled frown.

"He has left," said the nun. "In a word, he has fled. We do not know where he is, and we are very, very worried."

It is gratifying to note that the criminal work of the [lynch]
mob murderers . . . has declined in 1899, being much smaller
than in any year since 1885.

—The South Bend
Tribune, January 1, 1900

ister Mary Elizabeth insisted that Hilda be driven back to
South Bend. "It isn't any trouble at all," she replied when
Hilda protested. "Several of us are going in to town, for a
concert at St. Patrick's. Only in one of the farm wagons, so you
mustn't expect luxury, but there's plenty of room. It'll save you
time, and you look as if your feet hurt."

Hilda admitted to having a blister, and then suddenly smiled.
"I never before understood that nuns were so—so real, so human!
I did not imagine you ever thought about things like feet."

"Goodness, child, I'm a teacher, or I used to be. I've been on
my feet all day long for many years, surely enough to know about

blisters. And speaking of homely matters, I imagine before you undertake a journey in a bouncing wagon, you might like to visit . . ." She nodded at the door. "It's down the hallway, to your right."

Hilda blushed and accepted the proffered hospitality with alacrity.

"Sister Mary Elizabeth, you have been so kind. I do not know how to thank you," she said when she came back, "but there is one thing still. I do not know if I should ask, but is it allowed that I see the priest Mr. Kee visits— visited?"

For the first time, the nun looked uncertain. "Why, my dear?" she asked, frowning a little.

Hilda was taken aback. "Because—I wish to ask him—I wish to know—I am concerned—," she stammered.

The nun appeared to make a decision. "His name is Father Zahm," she said slowly. "He is accompanying us to the concert. He is a scientist, and not"—she hesitated, choosing her words carefully—"not always an easy person to talk to. I understand, I believe, your need to know about Mr. Kee. You are connected with this affair, and have a fellow feeling for the man, since he, too, is a foreigner. Father Zahm—" She stopped, seeing the look of dismay growing on Hilda's face.

"I'm talking too much," she said with a little smile. "Come, or we'll be late. Ask Father Zahm your questions, but be prepared for short answers."

The concertgoers packed into the wagon, somewhat uncomfortably. Sister Mary Elizabeth made sure Hilda, on one of the bench seats next to several young nuns, was seated directly across from an aloof, austere-looking man of about fifty, and introduced them.

"Father Zahm, this is Hilda Johansson. She is the young woman who discovered the body of Miss Harper, and she would like to ask you some questions about Mr. Kee."

With that, the nun settled back on her own seat and left Hilda to her fate.

"Yes?" said Father Zahm without a hint of a smile.

Hilda raised her chin. She, too, could be aloof and direct. "I wish to know where he might be."

"And why do you want to know that?"

His voice was sharp; Hilda, wary of a Catholic priest to begin with, felt her heart beat faster. "I—I am afraid for him," she stammered. "He is foreign. The police—"

"Young woman, I don't know what business it is of yours, but I have no idea where Mr. Kee might be. I scarcely know him. He came to me because he had known a friend of mine, a brother priest, in China. He was very foolish to run away, but I haven't the slightest notion where he went."

He turned his head away, but Hilda couldn't leave it at that.

"But he did spend the day here? The day Miss Harper was killed?"

Father Zahm's countenance grew so forbidding that Sister Mary Elizabeth felt obliged to intervene.

"Miss Johansson has a personal interest in the matter, Father. It was her unfortunate fate to discover Miss Harper's body."

"Hmph! I fail to see, logically, why that circumstance should lead to her wishing to meddle. However, it is certainly true that Mr. Kee was at the college last Wednesday, in my rooms for most of the time. I told the police that, but they are as illogical as most people." He glared at Hilda and took out of his pocket a breviary in which he proceeded to bury himself. Even Hilda dared not ask him any more questions.

His cold manner cast a pall on the spirits of the whole party. No one said another word all the way to Tippecanoe Place. The driver left Hilda at the foot of the back drive, and the horse clopped off down the street, iron-shod hooves and wheels ringing on the brick pavement.

She toiled up the drive, footsore and discouraged. She had walked for miles, been scared out of her wits more than once, and for nothing. No one would help her. No one would help Mr. Kee. Norah was right. This was the way America was, and no one person was going to change any of it, especially not one as unimportant as Hilda Johansson.

She rounded the corner of the house.

"And it's about time you showed your face, me girl! Where have ye *been?*"

Patrick stood in her path, feet planted firmly, arms crossed, face red with annoyance.

It was the last straw. Her face crumpled; tears rolled down her cheeks. "Oh, Patrick, it has been—I am—" Sobs choked off her voice.

"Here, now!" he said in astonishment. "And what is it, then? Sit down, darlin' girl, and tell me."

Blinded by tears, she allowed him to lead her to a bench under a tree, where she sat and sobbed to his soothing murmur of meaningless words, until the sobs diminished to sniffles and she reached in her pocket for a handkerchief.

"Ah!" she said sharply, and drew out her hand. It was bleeding from a cut.

"Oh, it is the glass! I forgot—and the wagon ride—"

She dissolved again. Patrick patiently handed her his own handkerchief and waited.

"All right, are ye?" he asked when the storm seemed finally over.

"All right," she replied in a small voice.

"Will it all start up again if ye tell me what it's about?" he asked doubtfully, the eternal male treading warily near the unpredictable female.

"No. I do not think so."

"Well, then, what's this about a glass?"

Hilda took a deep, shuddering breath and got herself under command. "It is a place to begin, *ja*." She related her journey, telling about the kind family on the porch, and fretting over the broken glass.

"They are not rich, Patrick, it is a thing that will worry them, and I have no money to replace it—"

"Never mind. If me mother has one she can spare, I'll give it to you. If not, I told you I have some money put by. Go on."

She told it haltingly. She skimmed over her foolish fears, but Patrick seemed to understand.

"Ah, and it's a brave thing ye did, girl, to go all the way out there, and scared as ye are about the priests and all!"

"It was not just the priests," she said in a burst of candor. "There was a graveyard. And it was very foolish, but I was afraid." She looked up at him, ready to be defensive. "There are *spökes*, sometimes—ghosts—I do not know what you call them in English. But they live in woods, and perhaps around graves, and they are good sometimes, but very bad at other times—" She waved her hands in the air, helpless to explain the deep-rooted folklore of her people.

"Like the little people of Ireland, I expect," said Patrick without a hint of a smile. "And little people or not, it's not a good thing, a graveyard, not to come upon all unknowin', like. You were brave," he repeated. "Well, and so you went to Notre Dame."

She told him the whole story, the kindly nun, the cold, distant priest, and the hunted Mr. Kee.

She was composed as she finished. The storm of weeping, and Patrick's sympathy, had done her good, washed away the emotions of several trying days and left her calm, but exhausted.

"So you see," she concluded, "that it is very bad for Mr. Kee. And I think he made it worse when he ran away."

Patrick shook his head dolefully. "It's a bad thing all round. Though the police won't be so quick to arrest him, now the good fathers have said he could not have done it."

Hilda's lip curled a bit at "good fathers." "I did not like him," she said flatly.

"Father Zahm? He's important, all the same. He's a famous professor, did you know?"

"No." *And I don't care*, her manner implied.

"Well, he is. Some say he's the most important man at the university, barrin' Father Morrissey, o' course. I've never met him, meself, though I've heard he's not the most patient of men. But if he says a thing is true, it's true. Even the police know that."

Hilda sat, brooding. Finally she sighed deeply. "This is very bad, Patrick."

"It is," he agreed. "The poor man isn't in danger from the police anymore, but—"

"Patrick! How can you say that? He is in very great danger, and so am I. And so, maybe, are you."

"But if they know he couldn't have done it—"

"Oh, you are so innocent, Patrick!"

The young man frowned, his mustache turning down. If there is one thing a man does not like to be called by a woman, it is innocent.

"Look!" Hilda insisted. "Now the police know Mr. Kee could not be guilty. But do you not see who that gives them as the best suspects?"

"No," said Patrick with a surly grimace.

"The Harper family, of course. And they will not want it to be the family, nor even any of her friends, because they are important people. So they will pay no attention to the evidence and try to arrest Mr. Kee anyway. Or else—or else, Patrick—they will decide it was one of us!"

Patrick absorbed what she had said. He hated to be shown up, but he was fair-minded. Hilda was right. He nodded, then groaned.

"And that might not even be the worst of it, me girl."

"What do you mean?" she asked, her voice rising with apprehension.

"Even if we should all be safe from the police—and probably we're not, as you say—even then— you'll not go all wobbly on me again, will ye?"

"No, but tell me!"

"Well, then—if the papers get hold of this, or rumors get around town—then, don't ye see, we could be in great danger."

"I don't understand."

"From the people, girl! Do ye know how many lynchings there were in this country last year?"

... in order to enjoy the inestimable benefits that the liberty
of the press ensures, it is necessary to submit to the inevitable
evils that it creates.

—Alexis de Tocqueville,
Democracy in America,
1835

Hilda did not "go all wobbly," but only her pride and her Swedish stubbornness kept her from it. She bit her lip and clenched her fists, her fingernails digging hard into her palms, until she could trust herself to speak.

"He did not do murder, Patrick." She spoke quietly. "I do not like Father Zahm, but I do not think he would lie. And I am sure Sister Mary Elizabeth would not. And neither did we kill, either of us. And we are all in danger."

She sat in silence for a moment, looking at her hands. "Patrick. We cannot escape what this means."

He looked at her, his mustache drooping.

"If Mr. Kee did not murder Miss Harper—and he did not—we know who probably did. What are we to do about it?"

Up until that moment Patrick's concern had been to keep himself firmly out of what was becoming an increasingly awkward and dangerous business. He had been prepared to argue with Hilda, to invoke the spectre of Mr. Williams, if necessary, in order to keep her out of it, as well. They would have enough trouble simply defending themselves, if it came to that, without trying to do the job of the police for them. Hilda would rant and rage, but he had become adept at dealing with Hilda's temper.

What defeated him was her quiet assumption that he would help her. Against the trust in those blue eyes, he had no armor.

"I don't know," he said honestly. "Do you understand how dangerous this could be?"

"Yes. But there is danger in doing nothing, also. We must try to learn the truth, Patrick."

He sighed, studied his boots, and finally looked up at her. "Yes," he said.

Thus was the compact sealed.

Another silence fell. Hilda's face wore a look of fierce concentration, Patrick's of gloom.

When she finally spoke, her voice was still quiet, but charged with energy, like a muffled drum. "T'ree t'ings we must do." She frowned at herself and started over. "Three things." She ticked them off on her fingers. "We must try to protect Mr. Kee. That is first. Then we must try to find him. And the hardest thing of all, but the most important: We must try to find the real killer."

Patrick tried one last-ditch effort. "And why can't we leave that, at least, to the police? They're paid to protect us."

"And do you think they will?"

The question was unanswerable. Patrick shook his head wearily.

Hilda sat up briskly. "Do not look so tired, Patrick. The first thing we must do now; you must help." A thought struck her. "You do not soon have to go on duty, no?"

"Not until after supper. I got meself the whole day off because—oh, the saints preserve us!"

"What?" For he had sat bolt upright on the bench and smacked his head.

"I clean forgot, girl! At this very moment, I'm supposed to be playin' me fiddle at St. Pat's! That's why I was put out when you were late; there's a concert, and I wanted to take you, as a surprise. And then you put it right out of my head!"

"I am sorry, Patrick." Hilda looked at him contritely. "I knew about the concert, too, because the fathers from Notre Dame, and the sisters, drove me into town. They were to go to the concert, but I did not know you were to play. Is it too late?"

"Away and away too late. It's begun, now, and the Irish songs were the first on the program. Oh, don't look so sad, darlin'. I was only one of the fiddles; they'll never miss me."

But Patrick would miss making his music, and Hilda knew it. Her heart smote her. "I am sorry, Patrick. If you want to go now, you might be able to play, later."

"And what about you?"

"Me, I must do many things. I cannot go."

"Well, then, there's no use cryin' over spilt milk, is there, now? And I'm not goin' to let you do whatever it is you're doin' on your own. I don't trust you not to be in trouble, you and that Swedish stubbornness. We'll go together to wherever you're goin'."

She stood up resolutely. "*Ja*, that is good. We must go to the newspapers."

"The newspapers! But I thought you were forbidden to talk to newspaper men. Mr. Williams—"

"I am. That is why you must be with me. And we will go *now*, please. I will explain as we walk."

Patrick looked at her. Never before had he allowed a girl to order him around as Hilda did. She was stubborn, arrogant, impatient, and entirely too eager to take the lead. If only she weren't so distractingly pretty . . .

"We'll go this second if you want, me girl," he said with a sigh.

"*Ja.* Come, then." She marched down the drive, trying not to wince when the blisters rubbed.

Patrick shook his head and followed.

"Now, Patrick," said Hilda, as they walked rapidly down Washington Street, "listen, and I will tell you what we must do."

"Yes, ma'am!" he said with a smart salute.

Hilda did not allow herself to smile. "We will go to the *Tribune*. That is the Republican newspaper, the one Mr. Clem reads; he does not approve of the politics of the *Times*."

Patrick, a devout Democrat and *Times* reader, snorted. "But it's an afternoon paper! If we go to the *Times* first, they'll print the story tomorrow morning."

Hilda shook her head firmly. "No. The *Tribune*. We go there because if Mr. Clem hears that I went to them—I hope he will not, but it is possible—he will not mind so much. And I must be very careful, because of Mr. Williams. It must look as though I am only there to accompany you; you must talk, Patrick."

"And are ye goin' to tell me what to say, Your Majesty? And why do ye never call me Pat?"

She ignored the side issue. "It is very easy. You will tell them what we know—that Mr. Kee is innocent, everything. Then, you will tell them that we go from there to the *Times*. And the *Tribune* will not like it that the other newspaper will print such an important story first, and they will put out a special edition. And people will know the truth much sooner, *ja?*"

Patrick, who had been growing more and more annoyed, now looked at her with open admiration. "You are a marvel, you are!" he said handsomely. "I would never ha' thought of it."

Hilda's smile, if a little tired, was also a trifle smug. "Now, Patr—Pat, this is what you must say . . ."

When they got to the *Tribune* offices, Hilda decided she would not go in with Patrick at all, but would wait in the anteroom. "For if you said the wrong thing, I would start to speak, and it would be very bad."

"Now, look here, if you've set your mind that I'm goin' in there to say wrong things—"

"Patrick! Keep your voice down. You will say the right things, but I will stay here."

She smiled at him, as brilliantly as she was able.

Her best smile was very good indeed. Patrick went in to beard the lions of the press while Hilda paced.

It seemed to Hilda that he was a very long time. When he finally came out, he was accompanied by two men, one in a tall silk hat. Hilda shrank back into a corner as the party swept out the door. She hesitated, pondering whether to follow, when the outer door opened again and Patrick, his finger to his lips, beckoned.

They turned right, not left, as they came out of the building—not back to Tippecanoe Place, but on downtown.

"But—," was all Hilda managed to get out.

"Shh!" Patrick steered her rapidly down the street until they had turned the corner onto Colfax.

"But we do not *really* go to the *Times!*" she protested.

"I know. It's the other way up the street, anyhow. I didn't

want you to say anything while those two could maybe hear you."

"Who were they?"

Patrick grinned. His cockiness had been completely restored. "The one in the topper was Mr. Miller, the editor of the *Tribune!*"

He had his satisfaction. Hilda's hand flew to her mouth and her blue eyes grew large. "Oh!" she breathed.

"And the other one was a reporter. They were going over to St. Pat's to find Father Zahm and Sister Mary Elizabeth."

"Patrick, stop! You must tell me everything."

"Sure," he said. "Here, what do you say we go back to the Oliver Hotel, and I buy you an ice cream sundae?"

"Patrick! We talk of murder, and danger, and you wish to eat ice cream?"

"Yes. And so do you. We can talk just as well in comfort, you know. And you can just taste it, can't you, all cold and creamy and sweet . . ."

Hilda was sorely torn. Ice cream was a rare treat, and she was so hot, but it didn't seem proper, and not only because of the frivolity. After all, a hotel? Unchaperoned? She had never set foot in the magnificent new hotel.

"I should not go there with you," she said, looking at her boots.

Patrick just looked at her. "This is the twentieth century, you know."

Hilda would rather die than be thought old-fashioned. She allowed herself to be persuaded.

Even as urgently as Hilda wanted information, it was some time before she could pay attention to Patrick, once they got to the hotel. The lobby overwhelmed her with its elaborate chandeliers, its gold trimmings, its allegorical paintings—the latter consisting of scantily clad ladies who brought a blush to her cheek. She was hesitant about climbing the stairway to the second floor.

"But, Patrick, that is where the bedrooms are," she whispered.

"Come on, darlin', that's where the dining rooms are, too. Do ye not trust me?"

"No," she muttered—but followed him up the gorgeous staircase, finer even than the one at Tippecanoe Place.

The main dining room was closed at that hour of a Sunday afternoon, but the smaller adjoining room was spectacular enough to bring a gasp to Hilda's lips. She suppressed it quickly and tried to look as if she were accustomed to being seated deferentially and waited on like a real lady.

"Thank you, Patrick," she said when she had finished the last creamy, cold, delicious spoonful of ice cream, had licked the last drop of dark, rich chocolate sauce from the spoon. "I think that was the best thing I ever have eat!"

"Eaten. And it's Pat, remember?" he said with a grin. "You're welcome. Now, down to business."

"Yes." She pushed her bowl away and leaned intently over the table.

"Well, I went in, and I asked for the editor. The man at the desk said he wasn't there, that nobody much was there, it bein' Sunday and all, when they don't put out a paper, and tomorrow's not due out for another twenty-four hours, near. So then I said I was pained to have bothered 'em, and I'd just get meself down to the *Times*."

He smiled reminiscently. "That got 'em, all right. The man rustled up a reporter for me, and I told him what you said. That Mr. Kee was innocent, and it could be proved. He wanted to know how I knew, and I just said I'd heard rumors, but if he talked to the people at Notre Dame, he'd find out for himself. I made them promise they'd print the story, and then I told them I was on my way to the *Times*."

Hilda laughed, a quiet, delicious little ripple. "What did they do?"

"*That* was when they figured out that the editor was there, after all. They called him down from his office, and he asked me a lot of questions, but I just kept on saying I'd heard rumors, and the people who told me made me promise not to tell. Which was true enough, darlin', exceptin' that there was only the one person."

"That was good, Patrick! Oh, I *cannot* call you Pat! I do not like 'Pat.' It sounds too much like Paddy, and that is what that sergeant called you. I did not like it! You are Patrick." She gave a sharp little nod. "But did they believe you?"

"They believed me enough that the editor himself decided to go and have a talk with Father Zahm," said Patrick grandly. "Oh, and they asked me why I wanted to tell me story to the *Times*, as well."

Hilda nodded. "I told you."

"You did. And I had me answer ready, that I was worried for the poor man, that he would be hunted down—oh, I sang it sweet for 'em. And that," he finished triumphantly, "was when Mr. Miller decided he'd put out a special edition!"

Hilda sighed luxuriously. "It worked!"

"There is just one thing," Patrick said, his voice a little less self-assured. "I hope you'll think I did right."

"What?" She was anxious.

"I didn't tell them me own name. I thought—well, I know well what me family would say if I got me name in the paper. Besides, though, there are people I know on the police who'd put two and two together and reckon you were the one as told me, and it might be bad for you. So I called meself Danny O'Reilly."

"Good. That was very good, Patrick. I did not think of that. You cannot get into trouble for lying to the newspaper, can you?"

"Hilda, me girl, if you could, half the politicians in this country'd be in jail half the time!"

Man has his will—but woman has her way!

—Oliver Wendell Holmes,
The Autocrat of the
Breakfast Table, 1858

Hilda smiled, showing her dimples, but she didn't laugh aloud. She and Patrick were tucked away in a corner, and no one in the crowded tearoom seemed to be paying any attention to them, but she still intended to be careful. If word ever got back to Gudrun that she had been seen with a man in the Oliver Hotel, she didn't even want to think of what would happen.

She settled her hat more squarely on her head and assumed a very serious expression.

"Now, Patrick. We have done—*you* have done what is possible to help Mr. Kee. For now. But I thought very hard about this. The next things, we must do quickly also."

Patrick's face took on a lively apprehension. It was never

very safe, with Hilda, to predict what "the next things" might be. "You're not goin' off to look for him, are you?"

Hilda looked surprised. "For why would I do that? I do not know the area well, and I do not have my time free. That is a silly idea, Patrick."

"I'm glad you think so. I think so, meself. Go on, then."

She shook her head. "Some of the time I do not understand your thought. My idea is this: Mr. Kee will be safe now, if the newspaper prints the story before either the police or a—a crowd, a—"

"A mob?" Patrick offered.

"Yes, that is the word. Not a good word, but the correct one. If the mob does not find Mr. Kee before they can read that he is innocent. *But.*" She emphasized the word and cupped her chin in her hands, gazing intently across the table at Patrick. "*But,* he will be safe only for a small time. Perhaps a day, perhaps two, longer if *Herre Gud* looks after him. After that, the mob—and the police, too, it is possible—will grow tired of waiting. They will decide that the fathers at Notre Dame are lying to protect him, and they will start to hunt him."

She looked at Patrick, her blue eyes bright with compassion. "He is a stranger here, Patrick. He knows no one except the fathers at Notre Dame, and them he knows only a little. And Notre Dame is the one place he cannot return. I feel so sorry for him."

If they had been alone, Patrick would have dared pat her hand. In a public place, he couldn't do that, but he smiled at her with all the warmth his Irish eyes could summon up. "You're a fine person, Hilda, and no mistake."

Hilda lowered her eyes modestly. "It is good of you to say so. So maybe you will not be angry if I say to you that the yob— the *job* of finding him must be yours."

Patrick frowned. "How d'ye see that?"

"You have the freedom. I do not. I must be at Tippecanoe Place, at my work, almost all of the time. Me, I can talk to other servants, I can learn things, and I can— can make the sum—can add—how do you say it?"

"Can put two and two together?" Patrick suggested, smiling in spite of himself.

"Yes, that is it! I can put two and two together." She nodded sharply, approving of the expression and tucking it away in her memory. "What I cannot do is go far, or talk to people I do not know. Especially men."

Patrick was frankly chuckling now. "Ye'd best not be talkin' to strange men, me girl!"

"Yes, that is what I mean," she said gravely. "But you can talk to anyone."

"Like who, for example? I can't just go runnin' around town askin' questions, ye know, me girl! I've got a job to do, as well as you."

"But it is a job where you spend many hours with nothing to do—"

"And the rest of the time workin' like the very devil, I'll have ye know!"

"Now, Patrick." She smiled at him with deliberate intent, her dimples showing to great advantage. "You should not swear, and anyway I do not believe the devil puts fires *out*."

It would have been fun to quarrel about it, but she wanted him in a good mood. "I know you work hard, but you still have much time to talk to the other firemen. And to the policemen, who are so near. And to the grocer and the butcher, when you buy food for the firehouse. And to your brothers. And Patrick . . ." She smiled again. ". . . you are so very good when you talk. You know you can make anyone do what you want them to."

"Except you. You never do what I want you to, at all, at all."

"That is not true!" It was a pained shout. At Patrick's raised eyebrows, she recovered herself and lowered her voice. "I come here, I eat ice cream, yes? I go with you on the river. I walk out with you, when everyone says I must not. So I think now you will do this for me, *ja?*"

He sighed dramatically. "I suppose so. So you want me to ask everyone I see if they've seen this fellow?"

"And have them ask others, and still others. You see, Patrick, it is the ordinary people, the poor people, who will know the places to hide. And you must not forget to tell that he is innocent. They will believe you, and they will try to find him, and when they do, they will not betray him."

"Hmph! Well, I'll try." But he was impressed, even though he tried to hide it. This girl had a mind to match her beauty. "And meanwhile, you're askin' every servant you know who killed Miss Harper? Doesn't seem to me they're likely to know."

"Of course they will not know. But they will know something. Servants always know more than the family thinks they know. And I will learn a thing here and a thing there and soon I will know all." She said it airily, with a wave of her hand.

"Hmph!" said Patrick again, with more genuine skepticism this time. "Think you're Sherlock Holmes, do ye? *I* think your heart is in the right place, but you're daft if ye think you're a detective. That's a dangerous job, a job for the police—"

At that her temper escaped. The feathers on her hat danced with her fierce impatience, and she had to struggle to keep her voice low. "Patrick, we have talked of this already! Do you *still* think so much of the intelligence of the police? Or of their goodwill? You, an immigrant yourself!"

Patrick bit his lip. There was truth in what she said, but— "All right! They're maybe not the smartest police force in the world. They maybe take a few bribes now and then, and they're not always fair to people like us. I'll grant you all that. But there's good, honest men there, too, friends of mine, and they're paid to do their job, and we're not. And I'll not be a party to lettin' you go off half-cocked and get yourself killed!"

"Patrick Cavanaugh, take me home!" She said it in a furious stage whisper and stood up, nearly knocking over her chair.

She was halfway down the stairs before Patrick could catch up with her.

"Just wait, then, can't ye? I have to pay the bill or they'll come after me. Don't ye go anywhere, do ye hear?"

She gave him no reply but an icy glare. He ran back, paid the bill with which an irate waiter was starting to pursue him, picked up his hat, and joined her—still waiting, but tapping her foot.

"What do you mean by runnin' out on me?" he demanded once they were safely on the sidewalk.

"And what do you mean, to break your promise?"

"What promise? I never promised I'd—"

"You did! You agreed we must do something. This is the something. If you will talk not so much and think more, you will see it is the only thing! If you will not help, I will do it myself, but it will be very much easier with your help. And do not, ever, ever, tell me what I may do!"

They quarrelled all the way back to Tippecanoe Place, a quarrel made the more heated by the need to conduct it in a furious undertone. The streets were now full of Sunday strollers, the ladies with their parasols, the gentlemen in top hats, and Patrick and Hilda were forced to pause at intervals, smiling fiercely at each other while they passed groups and couples, only to resume when they had a little privacy.

At last they arrived at the shady haven that was the Tippecanoe Place back drive, and Hilda plumped herself down on the bench near the back door. She had set a smart pace from the hotel, and her feet hurt her.

There was an awkward little silence.

"Me, I do not care what you decide to do," said Hilda at last. "I do what I think is right. If you will not help, that is your decision."

"For the tenth time, girl, it's not safe! For the one thing, ye might get yourself killed, and for the other, what if Mr. Williams finds out? Ye'd lose your job, sure, and then where'd ye be?"

"I will do nothing that I would not do in the ordinary. This is what I try to explain to you, only you will not listen! I will talk to my friends, as we do talk, when we work outside in this fine weather. I will talk to my sisters, who will tell me what the talk is in the houses where they work.

"You are not so stupid most times, Patrick. Can you not see that I can do this, and the police cannot? Servants will not talk to the police, but to me, one of them, they will say things. And I will put two and two together, and I will make of them a story—the story of what happened."

"Yes, and what miracle is goin' to make you able to do all these things?" Patrick jeered.

"The miracle has already been given," said Hilda in all seriousness. "It is my mind. I have a very good mind, Patrick. Of all my brothers and sisters, I am the quickest to learn—reading, writing, mathematics. And I learn English very quick, too, though it is such a difficult language. And I know, Patrick—not always, but almost always—I know what people think. I know when they lie and when they tell the truth. With my brothers and sisters, always I know."

Patrick was silent. He knew Hilda was intelligent, and it was true that she had mastered—well, *almost* mastered the English language very quickly. And he was uncomfortably aware that she often knew exactly what he was thinking, and was usually a step or two ahead of his more simple thought processes.

"Well," he said unwillingly, "supposin' ye *can* do all o' them wonderful things. What's goin' to keep ye from gettin' hurt? If what we think—if what *you* think is true, and it's . . ." He nodded his head significantly at the Harper house across the lawn.

Hilda sobered a little. "There is danger there, *ja*. But I will be careful. It is easier to keep the eyes open when you know where the danger is. And *Herre Gud*, he will look after me. You, Patrick, you will perhaps pray to your saints. That will not do any good, of course, but it will make you feel you are helping, and that will make you happier."

He couldn't help it; he shouted with laughter, and Hilda let her dimples show once more. "Now, Patrick, I must be quick, to change my clothes and go and talk to Annie, next door at the judge's house. She will come out at any moment, and I must not miss her. You will go and talk to people. Also, if you learn what the police think, you will tell me. And in turn, you will tell them what I learn, but with beautiful deceit, as you did today, so well! Go, Patrick! Come tomorrow at five o'clock, and we will talk!"

She grasped his hand for a moment, smiled, and dove down the basement stairs, heedless of her sore feet. Patrick, after a moment, took himself down the drive with the bemused look of a man who's been hornswoggled.

If a murder, anybody might have done it. Burglary or
pocket-picking wanted 'prenticeship. Not so murder. We're
all of us up to that.

—Charles Dickens, *Our
Mutual Friend*, 1865

s Hilda came through the back door, she stepped hard on a
blister, winced, tripped, and stumbled nearly into the arms
of Mrs. George.

"Oh, madam! I am sorry, madam, I—"

"Don't worry, my dear; it isn't your fault. I've invaded your
part of the world. I was looking for the lobsters that I asked Mrs.
Sullivan to cook for me. Where would they be, do you know?"

"Lobsters, madam?" Hilda, in her confusion, sounded as
though she had never heard of the creatures before.

"Yes, I'm having a few guests in tonight and I want to make
some lobster à la Newburg." She smiled at the expression on

Hilda's face. "I'm quite handy with a chafing dish, you know. I would have thought the lobsters would be in the icebox, but somehow I can't find them."

Hilda's mind cleared. "Oh, yes, madam, I remember now. Cook shelled them and chopped up the meat this morning after breakfast." She moved into the kitchen, Mrs. George following her.

"You're looking very pretty, Hilda—nice bright color to your cheeks. An afternoon out with your young man?"

"Yes, madam, thank you." The flush on her cheeks deepened a little as she opened the icebox door and found the bowl, covered with a plate. If only Mrs. George knew what kind of an expedition she and her "young man" had just had! "Here is the lobster."

Mrs. George took the bowl. "Thank you for your help, Hilda. Enjoy the rest of your Sunday."

Hilda curtsied, a protocol she had entirely forgotten earlier, and accepted her dismissal. Mrs. George made for the front of the house, Hilda for the service stairs.

Once upstairs she changed with lightning speed into her uniform, clucking sadly over her white skirt and waist. The day's activities had not been kind to them. They were streaked with the dust of the road, and some of the lace had caught on something. Luckily, white muslin would bleach nicely in the sun, and the lace was not torn, only ripped away from the skirt. She folded the garments over her arm and ran downstairs with them to the laundry. There, with as much haste as was consistent with care of the precious clothes, she washed and rinsed them, squeezing out as much water as she could, and headed outside with them, a few clothespins tucked into her apron pocket.

The clothesline kept for the servants' personal use was near the carriage house, uncomfortably close to the lilac hedge of terror-stricken memory. However, it was also immediately adjacent to the gate into the Harper property and the small area, devoted to nothing in particular, where Annie sat in an old wicker chair with her boots off, taking her ease as she did late every Sunday afternoon.

"Hello, Annie. I hope you had a good day, despite every-t'ing." Hilda stuck the clothespins in her mouth and began to hang up her dress, smoothing out the flounces as she went.

"Huh," replied Annie. "Depends on what you call good. Mrs. Harper, she called in an Irish girl to help, so I could get my time off. I told her, I says, 'I'm not a black slave, and if I can't get my time off, I can get a better job somewheres else,' I says."

"That is good," said Hilda with an approving nod. "You must stand up for your rights." She longed to ask Annie questions, but she had to get her in the right mood first, and she had to step gingerly. Danger might be very near.

"Rights, huh! You think so!" Annie replied sourly. "I got no rights where my family is concerned, I guess. I had to spend my whole day with my ma, and she gets crankier every week, it seems like. Today it was her leg. Hurt her so much she couldn't hardly get up to do nothin', accordin' to her. Had me waitin' on her hand and foot. As if I didn't get enough of that all week long, that I should have to do it on my day off, too!"

Hilda barely listened. Annie's litany of tribulations with her aged mother was all too familiar. "Did you cook the dinner, also?"

"Now, see, that's another thing. Hurtin' too bad to get out of her chair, she says, but when it comes to her stomach, she can take the trouble. Fried chicken and fixin's, garden sass, cold slaw, apple pie—oh, she cares enough about what goes into her mouth."

"It sounds good," said Hilda, who hadn't had a proper meal since breakfast.

"Huh! Enough to give me indigestion all night, I expect.

That's a purty thing you're fussin' with, but it's got tore. Was it that Patrick you go around with? Did he try to take liberties?"

Annie, a middle-aged spinster, was always avid for tales of Hilda's goings-on with Patrick, and was always disappointed when Hilda had none to report. Someday, Hilda thought, she would make up a mild kiss or two, just to give Annie a thrill. Not today, though. There were far more important things to talk about.

"No, I went for a long walk, out into the country, and the lace must have caught on a bush." More likely on the seat of the wagon, she thought, but she didn't have to tell Annie everything.

Annie pounced on that. "A walk? On a day when you could fry an egg on your hat? How come you didn't go to your sisters' house, like always?"

Hilda had been trying to manufacture an opening for her real topic. Here it was.

"Freya and Gudrun and Sven, they wanted to talk about— well, about things that were hard for me. I did not want to eat with them. Oh, Annie, it has been terrible, about poor Miss Harper, not knowing who did this thing! I do not know how you have been able to stay so calm!"

Annie shuddered and moaned to great effect. Here was a topic after her own heart, full of gloom and horror, with the opportunity for a full disclosure of her own sufferings. "Calm! If you'd seen my palpitations when they told us . . . well, I thought my last day had come, sure as you're born." She had forgotten that her first reaction had been a sense of grievance, not of grief. "Come and set a spell, Hilda. It gives me a crick in my neck to look up at you."

Hilda seized the invitation with alacrity. She stepped through the gate into the next yard and perched on an old bentwood rocker of remarkable discomfort.

"So you were upset," she prompted.

"Upset! Huh! How would you be if they told you someone from your very house was lyin' there dead 'n' cold, her face battered to a pulp . . ."

Even Annie, absorbed as she was in her narrative, couldn't help noticing the delicate shade of green creeping over Hilda's face. She stopped and coughed, though it wasn't in her to apologize.

"Um. I guess you know all about that. Well, anyway, I took a turn, and I ain't like to of recovered from it yet. Course, I can't get away from it, can I? Not with the whole family talkin' about it. Not that I pay any mind to what they say, but you can't help hearin', can you?"

"What do they say?" asked Hilda, who was feeling grateful, now, that she had eaten little that day. In fact, that ice cream sundae . . . better try not to think about it. She was getting close to some real information. "Do they have ideas of who did the terrible t'ing?"

"The judge, he don't say, just sits there lookin' like the wrath o' doom. Mrs. Judge, she thinks it was a foreigner, prob'ly one of them heathen Chinese. Mr. James, he thinks it was one of them tramps, and Miss Harriet and Miss Tricia, they just goes around cryin' when they're here. If you ask me, I think they're the only ones sorry she's gone. They set great store by their aunt Mary, though she was hardly never home.

"I heard Miss Harriet—well, Mrs. Stone, I s'pose I should say—she was talkin' to Miss Tricia—I mean, Mrs. Reynolds—about when they was little girls, and Aunt Mary took 'em to the circus. They talked like it was the best time they ever had in their whole lives. Their mama didn't think it was right, but she's such a sour old thing, she don't think nothin' is right if it makes you happy.

"That I will say for Miss Harper, even after she got religion and decided she was goin' to be a missionary, she didn't think you was goin' straight to the devil if you had a little fun."

Unexpectedly, Annie sighed. "I reckon I'm goin' to heaven, sure, 'cause I ain't never had no fun in all my life. I'd sure like to, before I die, even if Mrs. Judge fired me."

Hilda was suddenly filled with pity. "Annie, come out with me one day. Wednesday is your day, too, is it not? We could have some fun together."

Annie slipped her feet back into her boots and stood up. "Ooh! My feet have swelled up on me somethin' awful! That's right nice of you, Hilda, I'll say that, but it don't show good sense. You know I got to look after Ma in my time off, only if I can't 'cause I got to work."

"Lie," suggested Hilda. "Send your mother a message. Tell her you must work. Then come out with me. She will never know."

Annie looked really shocked. "Sakes alive, child, I couldn't do that! S'posin' she had a bad spell, and died! I'd never be able to look myself in the face again. The idea!" She scuttled away to the house, as though afraid Hilda might persuade her, and Hilda shook her head at her own ineptness. She had used up an opportunity to talk to Annie and had learned nothing except that the judge "looked like the wrath of doom."

The information strengthened her suspicions, but did nothing to help her obtain any proof.

HILDA HAD TO fight to keep herself awake after her solitary supper, eaten in the kitchen. It had been a long, eventful day, and she had walked miles, but there was still something she must do. Slipping a few coins into her pocket, she waited until Mr. Williams had retired to his chair with his pipe and the latest *McClure's Magazine*, and then crept out the back door and up the steps, moving around the back of the house until she could lean, unobserved, against the foundation of one of the porches.

The rough-dressed stone made an uncomfortable backrest, which was probably just as well. The evening was soft and peaceful. Somewhere tiny tree frogs were peeping; pairs of mourning doves exchanged their last sleepy coos.

Other animals were abroad in pairs as well. She heard the yowl of an amorous tomcat and the hiss and scream of an apparently scornful female. That set a dog barking until the bang of a screen door indicated that Rover was safely inside for the night.

Then there was silence, warm silence filled with the scent of new-mown grass and lilacs and irises and mock orange. No wheels rumbled on the brick pavement, no shouts of children disturbed the Sunday evening hush.

Hilda's head nodded. She jerked it up and stretched stiffly. She was going to have a few sore muscles tomorrow, and she longed for her bed. Soon, she would have to go in regardless; Mr. Williams would be locking the doors when it was full dark, and there were not, now, many minutes to go.

Ah! Was that—it was! In the distance, the cries of the newsboys began. "Extra! *Tribune* extra! Read all about hunted man! Extra!"

She ran as fast as she could run, blisters or not, and reached Main Street just in time to intercept one of the boys and buy a *Tribune*. The fading light made the small print hard to read, but she scanned the front page under a streetlight until she was sure that not once was her name mentioned, and that the account was fairly accurate. Then she ran back to Tippecanoe Place and slipped back into the house and into the servants' room.

"Excuse me, please, if I am not to come in here still," she said to Mr. Williams, "but I went out for the fresh air and heard the newsboys. There is an extra edition of the *Tribune*. I bought it for you; I thought it might be important." She handed it to him with an air of great innocence.

"Thank you, Hilda," he said stiffly. "That was thoughtful of you. How much was it?"

"Two cents."

He fished in his pocket, handed her two pennies, and frowned at the newspaper.

"Hmm. Have you read this?"

"No, sir." Well, it was almost the truth.

"It says the police are on the trail of a Chinaman for the murder of Miss Harper. Makes sense."

Hilda bit her tongue and waited for him to read further.

"Ah. It seems the police are wrong, at least according to this. Says the Chinaman couldn't have done it if he was where people say he was."

He read a few more lines, then stood up with decision. "I must take this upstairs. Mr. Clem and Colonel George will wish to read it when they return, if they have not already done so. You did well, Hilda, but I think I will not give it to you to read when they have finished. You have been quite stimulated enough by this matter, though I will say you have been behaving yourself reasonably well the past day or two. You may resume your normal—er—habits tomorrow. Good night, Hilda."

And he took the paper off to iron it and set the ink before taking it upstairs.

Your bait of falsehood takes this carp of truth; And thus do we . . . By indirections find directions out.

—William Shakespeare,
Hamlet, 1600–1601

he next morning, Hilda, having slept nearly as soundly as poor Miss Harper, woke well before five. She washed and dressed as silently as she could, leaving her boots off until she had descended one flight of stairs. Her feet, still slightly swollen, didn't want to be buttoned up, but she persevered, then tiptoed down the bare wooden service stairs to the first floor.

It would be in either the library or Mr. Clem's study. She tried the study first; it was the nearest. She didn't dare light the gas yet; she shouldn't be tidying this part of the house for another half hour, at least, and she couldn't risk anyone seeing the light. But she could open the draperies, very quietly. Dawn was a few minutes past; by its pearly light she could just see that the desk was clear, and no papers lay on the tables.

She made her way, more or less blindly, through the inner corridor to the great hall, drew the draperies there, and went into the library.

This was her favorite room in the house. Its hexagonal shape was unusual, but interesting, and there was something about all the warm mahogany in the bookcases and the fireplace that felt friendly and comfortable. On days when she was well ahead with her work, she liked to linger here, touching some of the books that had been left lying on tables, running her duster lovingly along the elaborately carved overmantel, occasionally reading a line or two, if a book had been left open, before she inserted a bookmark and closed it neatly.

Today she wasted no time, but opened the draperies and looked around her in haste. And there—yes, there was the extra edition, lying folded on the big desk in the center of the room. She snatched it up and took it to the window, an eastern window, but there was too little light yet to read the small print. With a small exclamation of Swedish wrath, she looked around the room.

The coal box, that was it. She opened the polished mahogany door in the fireplace surround that concealed, in the winter, storage for the day's supply of coal to feed the fire. In summer it was empty and clean. She had thought Mr. Williams overparticular to insist that the box be thoroughly cleaned for the summer. Now she was grateful for his persnickety nature. She put the folded newspaper carefully in the box, eased the door shut, and stood with a sigh of relief. There would be plenty of time to read the paper before the family came down, now that it was safely out of Mr. Williams's reach.

The morning *Times* was her other immediate concern, but there was no use looking for it yet. The newspapers were not delivered until around six o'clock. She would simply have to organize her work so that she was very near the front door when it arrived. And that meant getting a few things out of the way first.

It was safe now to light the gas in the reception room next to the front door, and begin her morning chores. She went about her duties with the speed born of familiarity. Open the windows to their widest, shake and beat dust out of the draperies. Sprinkle the carpets with old tea leaves, then sweep them with pan and brush. Dust the furniture and woodwork with a feather duster, dust the ornaments (very carefully) with a soft cloth, wash dust and soot off the windowsills. And all the while Hilda was thinking of what she must do today to forward her ends.

She would have little free time, for several house guests were arriving tonight to stay for a few days. Decoration Day was Wednesday, and that meant important events, this year especially. James Oliver, South Bend's other great captain of industry, was, in the evening, to be presented with a huge gold loving cup in honor of his many contributions to the welfare of South Bend, especially his splendid new hotel. It was to be a great surprise; Mr. and Mrs. Oliver knew nothing of what was coming, but since Mr. J. M. Studebaker had originated the idea and Colonel George was on the committee, the Tippecanoe Place staff knew all about it. That, Hilda thought, might well be the time Judge Harper would choose to announce his candidacy for Congress, if he still intended to do so. Hilda had her own ideas about that, but if he decided not to announce, after all, that would create a stir, too.

But holidays, however exciting, meant extra work in preparation and cleaning up afterward. Hilda sighed rebelliously as she rubbed at a stubborn smudge on the drawing room mantel. Why was it that extra work always came just when she wanted a little time to herself?

She snatched a few minutes, as soon as there was enough light, to read the extra edition carefully. It didn't take her long. Only the front page had new material; the rest was simply Saturday's paper, recopied. There were a few inaccuracies, but on the whole the *Tribune* had done exactly as she had hoped. Mr. Kee (once referred to as Mr. Lee) was depicted as an injured innocent, and the police as overly eager to make an arrest. Hilda was relieved that the editor hadn't come right out and called the superintendent of police incompetent; the anger such an accusation would generate could only make matters worse. A plea for calm reason set the right tone, suggesting moderation without mentioning—and so bringing to mind—its opposite.

Very good. It wasn't enough to contain the situation for long, but as a temporary measure, it satisfied Hilda. She put the extra edition back very carefully, exactly where she had found it.

A tuneless whistle, gradually growing louder, finally penetrated her consciousness. The newsboy was crossing the front lawn on his way to deliver the paper. He would have to choose this morning to whistle! Hilda could not open the great front door, of course; Mr. Williams was the keeper of the house keys. She leaned perilously out one window and called, "Boy!" in a low but urgent tone.

Whistling too loudly to hear, he was about to pass the window. In desperation, Hilda snatched up her dustpan and threw it. It landed with a clatter on the stone walkway under the window, and the boy was brought up short.

"Hey! Whatcha throwin' things at me for?"

"Do not *shout!*" hissed Hilda. "You must not make so much noise. Mr. Clem, he does not feel so well," she improvised, "and we do not want to wake him. Please give the newspaper to me."

The boy shrugged, walked over to the high window, and, standing on tiptoe, managed to hand the paper to Hilda.

"And my dustpan, please," she added loftily.

"Huh! You threw it out, you get it back." The boy stuck his tongue out at her and sauntered down the drive. He did, however, forebear to whistle until he had attained the street.

Hilda stamped her foot, winced, and let the matter go. She could go out later to retrieve the dustpan. Meanwhile, the front page!

A quick glance told her that the *Times* had done little more than reprint what the *Tribune* had said last night. No significant additions, and most important, no mention of one Hilda Johansson or any version of that name.

Good! Now to get the paper down to the back door where it belonged, before Mr. Williams caught her.

It was a near thing. If Hilda's skirts had been more fashionably cut, close-fitting from waist to hips, she would have been caught. As it was, when she came out at the bottom of the service stairs and nearly ran into Mr. Williams, who was headed for the back door, it was only an instant's work to whisk the newspaper into her large petticoat pocket, where the fullness of skirt and apron concealed it completely.

"Good morning, Hilda," said the butler.

"Good morning, Mr. Williams. Are you ready to unlock the back door? I must go out for a moment and get some clothes I left out to dry."

"Certainly, but mind you hurry. There is a great deal to be done today." He opened the door, failed to see the paper at the bottom of the steps, and frowned. "That newsboy gets more and more careless every day. Now I suppose I'll have to look in the shrubbery."

"I will look, Mr. Williams. There is no need for you to climb all those stairs."

She was up the stairs in a flash, and called down, "Here it is, under a bush." She pulled it out of her pocket and tossed it down the steps to Mr. Williams, who caught it, muttering something about ". . . wrinkled and torn, as well!"

Hilda let her breath out soundlessly and went to fetch her clothes, not forgetting the dustpan.

Throughout breakfast she was unusually silent. Norah, who was pining to talk to her after several days of enforced silence, nearly made a remark about the cat and Hilda's tongue, but remembered in time the reception afforded the last such remark. "Are ye well, then?" she demanded instead.

"I am well, yes, thank you. I think hard, that is why I do not talk."

"And what are ye thinkin', that makes such a frown on yer face?"

Too late, Hilda saw the trap. "I think of my work, of course. There is much to do."

Norah looked at her suspiciously, but Hilda was not yet ready to take anyone but Patrick into her confidence. Later, if it became necessary. For now, she would keep her own counsel. So she smiled at Norah and asked her to pass the butter.

But her thinking, through the next few hours of work, bore fruit.

She had only two resources at her command that were of any use in investigating the death of Miss Harper. One was the servants' grapevine. The other was Patrick. Patrick had been assigned his task. Now it was her job, as she saw it, to learn all she could, as quickly as she could, about the movements of everyone in the neighborhood on the day of the murder—Miss Harper's family, her friends, all who might know where she went and whom she saw that fateful day. Of course, not all her friends might live around here. She, Hilda, had no idea what friends the lady had. But the family would know, and the family all lived within a few blocks.

The Harper house next door was the critical one, but though Hilda had in Annie an invaluable contact there, Annie was not discreet. Hilda would have to think out a method of approach that would give Annie just enough information to make her act, but not enough for danger.

Then the two nieces, Mrs. Reynolds and Mrs. Stone, lived, respectively, next door on the Taylor Street side, and a block up the street. By the greatest of good fortune, Freya worked in the house next door to Mrs. Stone's. And of course Hilda knew Kristina, another Swede and the housemaid at the Reynolds house.

From those contacts, the word would be spread. A whisper here, while scrubbing down the front steps, a quiet word there, over the back fence, and soon the underground network of servants would be alive with gossip.

The watchword was caution. Danger lay on all sides, no matter how Hilda had downplayed it to Patrick. She must make sure no one in the Harper family learned of her activities. Also, word must not get back to Mr. Williams of what she was doing. Nor— she shuddered as she scrubbed the tiled floor of one of the bathrooms—must Gudrun find out.

Freya, now . . . Freya could probably be counted on for some real help. Hilda sat back on her heels and considered. Of all Hilda's siblings, Freya, a year younger, was the closest to Hilda in age, as well as in temperament. The two of them had gotten into many scrapes together when they were children. Freya could be trusted with almost the whole truth.

The trouble was, she was at least as stubborn as most Swedes. Whatever she was going to do for Hilda, she'd have to think it was her own idea.

It was while Hilda was polishing the taps of the sink in the master bathroom that she had her idea, and as soon as she was able to leave her work for a moment she put it into action.

"Where are you going, Hilda? It's time to start setting the table for luncheon. Norah can't do it alone; there are ten guests."

"I go out to put these wet brushes in the sun to dry, Mr. Williams. I will be only a moment." Without giving the butler a chance to reply, she ran up the basement steps with a pail full of the brushes she had been using all morning, stubby scrub brushes, long-handled brushes for the water closets, stiff carpet brushes. The latter were seldom washed, but Hilda had taken a few minutes to rinse them out in a weak vinegar solution. It would give her another moment or two outside.

She scurried to the back of the carriage house and there, sure enough, was Annie, hanging out the laundry. It was one of Annie's perpetual grievances that, on laundry day, she was called upon to help the laundress.

It was all the opportunity Hilda needed. She knelt to spread her brushes on the grass, and gave vent to a loud, histrionic sob.

"Hilda?" Annie's voice was muffled through a mouthful of clothespins. "You cryin'? What for?"

"Oh, Annie!" (Another sob.) "I am so afraid! The police— they talk to me again. They think it was I who killed Miss Harper!"

Annie spat out the clothespins and stared avidly at Hilda. "No! Why'd they think a thing like that?"

"I do not know, I suppose because they are stupid."

"I thought it was that Chinese feller they were after."

"That is only a joke, a game, a—I do not know the word. They pretend to think that, so that I will make mistakes and they will catch me out." It wasn't very good, but it was the best Hilda had been able to come up with, and Annie wasn't brilliant. Hilda held her breath.

"You don't say!" An unpleasant thought penetrated Annie's sluggish mind. "You didn't do it, did you?"

"Annie! Of course not! But—but, Annie, I need your help. Can you learn for me where Miss Harper went and what she did that day—the day she was killed?"

"Yep. What for?"

"Because if I can learn for myself what happened, I can tell the police and they will not arrest me. But, Annie, above every-t'ing else, let no word reach Gudrun. She would worry. And oh, please, please, no one is to say anyt'ing to Mr. Williams. I would lose my yob!"

There was very real terror in those last words, and Annie nodded solemnly.

"I must go; he will be angry with me for being so long. Help me, Annie!"

And she was off, to wipe away the real tears that had flowed, and compose herself before Mr. Williams saw her.

In the childhood playacting in her family, Hilda had always taken the leading roles.

Crime brings its own fatality with it.

—Wilkie Collins, *The Moonstone*, 1868

ilda bolted her lunch that day in order to get back to her work. Sheets had to be aired for guest beds. Fresh towels had to be put out. Hilda and Norah between them had to wash vases, select a few of the flowers the gardener had cut, and arrange them nicely for the guest rooms. Mrs. Clem and Mrs. George would arrange the flowers for the dining table themselves.

It was mid-afternoon before all was done and Norah plodded up the stairs for her rest. "Ye comin' up then, Hilda?"

"Soon. I wish another spray of lilac for this vase."

"Looks good enough to me. I wouldn't think ye'd want to go near lilacs."

Hilda shrugged. She still wasn't quite ready to confide all the details to Norah. "Not the white ones, the purple, on the other side. Anyway, I do not have your Irish imagination, Norah."

She would, she thought as she slipped past the purple lilac hedge to the Reynolds house, have to remember to cut a spray to take in. At the back door, she knocked and asked for Kristina.

The butler looked at her condescendingly. "Kristina is not allowed visitors in her working time, Hilda. You ought to know that."

"It is a church matter, sir. I will not talk for long, but it is important."

He pursed his lips. Butlers were expected to uphold the morality of their underlings, and church was an important ally in that never ending battle. "Very well. But you may not come in. I will send her out to you. Be quick; she is very busy."

When Kristina came out, she was alive with curiosity. "What is it?" she asked in excited Swedish. "Has something happened? Mr. Blodgett said it had to do with the *kyrka*."

"That was an excuse. Now, listen, Kristina, this is important." And Hilda spun for Kristina much the same tale that she had used for Annie, without the hysterics. Kristina knew Hilda too well for those to be effective; moreover, she had not Annie's love of the sensational.

"I will do what I can," said Kristina doubtfully when she had heard Hilda out. "I do not want you to have trouble, but you understand I cannot ask questions openly."

Hilda understood Swedish caution, though she didn't always employ it. "I know. It is better that way. Keep your eyes and ears open, and tell me what you know, when you can."

"I will, Hilda. God go with you!"

She scampered back into the house, and Hilda flew down the street to the house where Freya worked. This was strictly forbidden during the day. She was not allowed to leave the grounds without permission. But the way she looked at it, this was her rest time. If she chose to spend it doing other things, what business was it of anyone else?

It was a little harder to gain an interview with Freya. The butler didn't know Hilda and was reluctant to let Freya come to the door for any reason whatever. As a last resort, Hilda dissolved into sobs, interspersing Swedish phrases with English words like "old mother" and "perhaps dying."

As she had expected, the man was completely unable to deal with a young woman's tears. He disappeared into the house, muttering, and after a moment or two Freya appeared at the back door, her brow creased with anxiety.

"Hilda. *Min syster!* What is the matter?"

"There is nothing the matter," said Hilda, in Swedish, through artistic sobs. "I had to talk to you, and tears were the only way I could get past that butler. Come out, under the tree, where I can talk to you without a sob every other word."

Freya suppressed a smile, and followed.

"Now. Listen well, I have little time. I wish to get information from all the servants about Miss Harper."

"Why?"

Hilda stamped her foot. "*Listen,* don't ask questions! I must know where Miss Harper went, what she did, and with whom, on the day she died. I have asked Annie to find out what she can, and Kristina, and I want you to ask the servants next door. I have told Annie it is because I am afraid for myself, that I think the police suspect me, but that is a lie. I tell you the truth so that you will not worry."

Freya opened her mouth, saw the look in Hilda's eyes, and shut it again.

"There are two important things. First, Gudrun must not know that I do this."

Freya nodded. "She would be very upset."

Hilda grimaced, making sure her face was turned away from the house, where a suspicious butler might be watching. "Upset" was a mild way of putting Gudrun's probable reaction. "And second, Mr. Williams must not hear anything of this. He has threatened me with the loss of my job if I continue to meddle in this matter, but meddle I must. Mr. Kee Long's life may depend on it!" And so might her own, but she judged it best not to tell Freya that.

"Oh, but he is not suspected anymore," said Freya. "The newspapers—"

"I was responsible for that, and it does not mean he is out of danger," Hilda interrupted. "I do not have time to explain; I must go. They do not know I am away. Keep your eyes and ears open and tell me what you learn!"

"How?"

It was a reasonable question, and Hilda had thought out the answer, but it was best to let Freya come up with the idea. "I do not know. You could write me a note, but I do not know where you would put it." She looked around, apparently aimlessly, and let her eyes rest for a moment on the line of large rocks that edged the lawn.

"I know!" said Freya. "There are rocks like that along your drive, the front drive, I mean. Tonight, on my way home, I will write a note and put it under the last rock, the one nearest the street, on the west side. I will write it in Swedish so that if anyone else finds it, they will not be able to read it. You will come out before you go to bed and get it. And if there is anything you need to tell me, you will leave it there for me. *That* will be our mailbox."

Her eyes sparkled. This was the kind of game she had loved as a child.

Hilda sighed inwardly. That was the danger with Freya, that she would forget this was not play, but deadly serious, and would let her sense of fun lead her into something foolish, or worse. It was a risk Hilda had to take.

"That is a good idea," she said warmly. "I must go now, or your butler will throw me to the *spökes*. You had better start to cry, and think of a really good story to tell him!" She embraced her sister hastily. "Thank you. I must be off!" They parted without so much as a wave; Hilda made sure to turn around artistically and give Freya one last longing look, and wipe away a tear, before turning away to walk down the street, head bowed. She did hope someone was watching.

She longed for her nap, but she wanted to check in with Annie, who might have learned something by now. She approached the great house with caution, in case Mr. Williams was looking for her, but he didn't seem to be outside. That was fortunate. She headed straight for the laundry yard, where her brushes should now be dry—and where she had the best chance of talking to her neighbor.

But Annie wasn't there. This was her usual time for a rest, as it was Hilda's, and always of a nice afternoon she could be found dozing in the wicker chair. Today, of all days, she was nowhere to be seen. Hilda lingered a few minutes, picking up her brushes and examining each one minutely to make sure it was dry, but no one from the Harper house appeared.

Pastor Forsberg would not have approved of the words that crossed her lips as she picked up the pail of brushes and went inside, entirely forgetting to pick any lilacs.

Once in her bedroom, Hilda fell asleep instantly, and woke only to Norah's voice, saying cautiously, "Hilda? It's near four-thirty, and there are eighteen people for dinner."

She yawned. She had slept for only half an hour, but she felt better. "T'ank you, Norah. I will be down in a moment."

She rinsed her face with cold water, put on a clean apron, her cap, and her boots—detestable things!—and plodded down the stairs to help Norah with the dinner table.

She was careful, though, to listen for the chimes of the big clock, and when it struck five she excused herself and ran outside to see if Patrick was there.

He was waiting for her at the top of the basement steps, and with a face as foreboding as thunder.

"Patrick! Somet'ing is wrong! The police—they have found Mr. Kee?"

"No, not that. Worse. You'd better sit down, me girl."

The only place to sit was on the top step. She dropped down to it, but her eyes never left Patrick's face.

"I do not know how to tell you," he said.

"Patrick! You frighten me!"

"I'm frightened meself, but for you."

"For me! Patrick, tell me! What have you learned? Has the mob taken Mr. Kee? Or—oh, no! You do not mean to tell me the police think that I—?"

Patrick shook his head and put his finger on her lips. "Hilda me girl, listen to me. You know that Wanda, the maid next door, has been missing for a couple of days?"

Hilda began to feel cold all over. "I knew that she had gone somewhere, that she had not come to work, but . . ."

She left the sentence unfinished and looked a question at Patrick.

He nodded. "She'd gone, all right. She'd gone into the river. Her body was found this afternoon at the boat landing at Leeper Park."

"I do not understand," said Hilda with a gulp. "She had gone to swim, and drowned?"

"She didn't drown. There was a cord around her neck. She was strangled."

It is stupidity rather than courage to refuse to recognize
danger when it is upon you.

—Arthur Conan Doyle,
"The Adventure of the
Final Problem," 1892

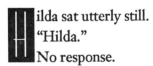ilda sat utterly still.

"Hilda."

No response.

"Hilda!"

"Quiet yourself! I t'ink!"

After another long moment of "t'inking," Hilda looked up
at Patrick and asked the last question he expected:

"Did she have a face?"

"Oh. Oh, I see. Yes, darlin', she had a face, no harm done to
it at all, at all."

"Because, you see, I dreamed . . ." She shuddered. "It is no matter. But I am glad that Wanda's face is still there." She studied her hands for a moment and then looked at Patrick again. "Patrick, was—do you know—Patrick, I did not . . ." She swallowed and continued. "I did not look at Miss Harper, after the first look, and I did not carefully read the accounts in the newspapers. How did she die?"

Reluctantly, Patrick nodded. "It's sorry I am to tell you, darlin', but she was strangled, too, with a scarf, they think."

"Then . . ."

"Yes. Probably the same person. And Hilda, me girl, that makes two women, both of them living next door—"

"Wanda did not live in. She boarded. I do not know where."

"All right," said Patrick impatiently. "Two women who spent most of their time next door to you, Hilda, in the very next house, and both of them murdered."

They looked at each other very soberly. There was a silence while each of them waited for the other to say it.

It was Hilda who spoke. "I was right, *ja?* Patrick, I—I did not want to be right. Such a family should not—such people should not—" Her feelings were too confused, too troubled to be expressed easily in an adopted tongue.

Patrick sighed heavily. "But it looks as though they are, and they did—one of them did."

"Will the police, now . . . ?"

"They'll not want to, sure enough. They won't want to believe someone in a judge's family could commit murder, any more than we want to believe it." There, it was said plainly, at last. "And they'll be afraid of what could happen. He's a powerful man, Judge Harper. And—Mr. Kee still hasn't been found. It'll be easy to blame him."

He paused, biting his lip, and when he spoke again his voice had changed. "Hilda, you don't like me tellin' you what to do, but I have to say this. It's time for you to start worryin', and takin' some care for your own skin . . ." He stopped, took Hilda's hand, and pressed it gently to his lips just as she heard Mr. Williams's outraged voice behind her.

"Hilda Johansson, come in here this minute!"

She snatched her hand away, her eyes furious. "Patrick Cavanaugh, you will never do such a t'ing again!" She marched off indignantly.

"The idea, coming out here for a flirtation when there is a dinner party, and Mrs. Sullivan in a state because the vols-au-vent didn't puff properly and she has to plan another hors d'oeuvre course . . ." Mr. Williams scolded her all the way down the stairs and into the house, changing his voice to a stifled whisper once they were within earshot of any possible members of the quality. Hilda was not allowed time to think, much less frame a reply, and it was several hours later before she realized that Patrick's quick thinking had saved her from a much worse fate. If Mr. Williams had thought they were talking about murder, instead of dalliance . . .

She sent Patrick a quick mental apology and turned back to handing round the whipped cream for Mrs. Sullivan's delicate chocolate mousse.

It was not until late in the evening, after dinner was over and the servants had eaten their own meal and were cleaning up, that Hilda had time to think about Patrick's shocking news. She had, in fact, preferred not to think about it. Murder—the murder of a fellow servant, by one of the gentry, probably by someone who lived next door, perhaps even by . . . but she didn't want to think about that either.

Poor Wanda! Hilda had barely known her, had spoken to her perhaps twice. Wanda was Polish, recently arrived in South Bend, shy, and not yet quite at home with the English language.

Then, too, she was so cowed by Annie that she had run like a startled rabbit every time the housemaid called her, so there had been no chance for real conversation.

But Wanda had been a servant and an immigrant like her, and now she lay dead, the second death in six days, and both of them committed by the same person, and that person almost certainly a member of Judge Harper's family, or else a close associate.

"Ye could've dried seven plates in the time ye've taken with that one," jeered Norah. "Tryin' to wipe off the pattern, are ye?"

Hilda jumped and nearly dropped the plate in question.

Two thoughts warred in her mind the rest of the evening. The first was that, as soon as the news went around—and that would be very soon, even though she had no intention of telling anybody—every servant in town would live in terror until the murderer was discovered, and Mr. Kee would be in terrible danger. Therefore the faster she could find out who was committing these terrible crimes, the better.

The second thought was that, no matter how high the stakes, she would much rather stay in the house, preferably with her head under the covers.

It took every bit of stubborn resolve Hilda possessed to sit up that night as Mr. Williams went around the house locking up. She waited until he had finished his chores and retired to bed. Then she waited longer, until the house was quiet.

It seemed to take forever. Some of the Studebakers' guests stayed up late, laughing and talking. Hilda didn't dare make her move until they had all retired for the night; someone might need something and ring for the butler. It was unlikely, but it was possible.

Then, too, she couldn't simply slip down the service stairs and sit in the kitchen until all was still. Mrs. George might take it into her head to prepare a midnight snack for someone, though *Herre Gud* knew they didn't need it after one of Mrs. Sullivan's "company" dinners.

But at last, at last, the lights were turned out, everyone was in bed and quiet, and Hilda could creep downstairs, carrying her boots.

The kitchen was stiflingly hot, and when Hilda stood on a chair to reach the window, she thought she might faint from the heat close to the ceiling. But the window opened easily, and the air outside was cool, with the smell of rain in it. That meant the heat might be breaking, thank goodness. She took a deep breath, like a drink of cool, sweet water, hoisted herself up onto the broad windowsill, and slithered through the opening.

The kitchen windows were farthest away from Mr. Williams's room three floors above; she had taken no chance of being heard. And she had chosen the window nearest the top of the steps that ran up the outside of the kitchen wall. It was only a shallow drop, but she had to land on the uneven stairs. The first foot to land slid off one step, and she would have tumbled down the whole flight if she had not managed to catch hold of the iron railing set into the wall and get her balance.

She wasn't hurt, but the fall had, to her ears, sounded very noisy. She crouched on the stairs, trying to hear over the pounding of her heart whether anyone was coming.

But there was no sound except that of the night insects and the little tree frogs, and gradually she regained enough courage to climb the steps and peek around as her head reached ground level.

There was nothing to be seen. The moon would rise later and would, anyway, be obscured by clouds. The only light came from the streetlamp on the corner, left burning all night in this wealthy part of town. It was an electric arc light, bright but very far away from the back door of the huge mansion on its expansive grounds. A bit of breeze had come up; the soft new leaves on the stately elm trees cast nervously moving shadows on the grass.

Hilda could not have said whether her stronger fear was of the dark trees and the trolls that just might live amongst them, or of the murderer who most certainly lived somewhere nearby. She took a deep breath to steady her ragged nerves and walked very quietly down the broad slope of lawn, avoiding the noisy gravel drive and resisting the urge to look over her shoulder.

At the bottom of the drive, the streetlamp was so much more effective that Hilda was glad she had left on her black uniform and taken off the white cap and apron. There was, unfortunately, nothing to be done about her white face and hands and bright hair. She stooped down quickly, her back to the light to hide her face as best she could, and lifted the last rock on the west side of the drive.

It was heavier than she had expected; she had to use both hands to lift it. She set it carefully on the grass and looked, with eyes and exploring fingertips, in the hole.

Her fingers met with scuttling things: slimy worms, and beetles and spiders that skittered away under her touch or crawled up her hand; she shuddered and stifled a squeal. But there was also a pale shape and the crackle of paper. She snatched it up, thrust it into her pocket, shook off the last crawling things with a final shudder of disgust, and stood.

Something cold touched her leg.

The only reason she did not scream was that there was no air in her lungs. She thought for a moment that her heart had actually stopped, but soon felt it trying to pound its way out of her chest. She drew a deep breath to scream for help.

The creature whined and snuffled, and put its head up to lick her hand.

"Rex!"

He gave a sharp little bark for the sheer joy of being spoken to, and nosed above Hilda's boot once more.

"I think," she whispered in Swedish, "that you have shortened my life by several years. Do not *ever* do that again!"

He whined and cocked his head at the unfamiliar, singsong speech, and Hilda recovered enough to remember her English.

"All right. That is a good dog. Now come back to the house with me, but *be quiet!*"

It was only with an effort that she restrained Rex's efforts to join her in her scramble back through the window, and she was glad of her forethought in choosing that particular window, far from the ears of authority. Rex was well-trained, moreover, and had long since been made to understand the need for quiet, especially near the house, on all occasions. He uttered one last disappointed whine as Hilda slithered inside and shut the window, and then, resigned, padded off for his nightly rounds, followed by a snooze in the stables.

As for Hilda, she stayed in the kitchen long enough to remove all traces of her illicit expedition and pilfer a fresh candle and a box of matches, then toiled upstairs to read Freya's note.

Give thy thoughts no tongue.

—William Shakespeare,
Hamlet, 1600–1603

Mr. Williams was very particular about candles. They were never to be used anywhere except on the dining table. It was explicitly forbidden to take them to one's room; for this reason, there were no candlesticks in the servants' bedrooms.

Hilda arranged the folding screen, which was wicker and light to move, so that it shaded her washstand from the door. Then she lifted the pitcher of water out of the basin, lit the candle, and dripped a little wax into the basin. She pressed the candle down into the hot wax, and, when it had set firmly, poured a little of the water into the basin as a precaution against fire.

Then she sat down to read.

The note was dirty from the earth, and closely written in very tiny handwriting. The candle flickered in the increasing draft from the open windows. Hilda strained her eyes.

My Dearest Sister, [she read in Swedish]
*I have had more time than usual for conversation, because
the family here were not at home all day today, and of course
next door is a house of mourning, with no entertaining and
only simple meals, so I was able to engage Luisa in a long
talk after our supper.*

Hilda sighed impatiently; the candle flame danced.

*Luisa serves as both housemaid and ladies' maid; it is a
small household. You may imagine that it took me some
time to bring the conversation to Miss Harper and the day
she died. Luisa was more inclined to talk of the difficulties
of looking after mourning costume, since Mrs. Stone had
but little black in her wardrobe and is obliged to make do
with only two changes of dress until more can be made. And
in this heat!*

Hilda gritted her teeth. Surely Freya would say something
that mattered, eventually?

*However, when I was able to turn her away from clothing,
I learned something VERY STARTLING! You asked
where Miss Harper went on that day. She came to visit
Mrs. Stone!*

Ah! Hilda turned the note over and held the paper closer to
the candle. The note was even dirtier on this side, and harder to
read. Hilda moved her face so near the flame that her hair was in
danger of catching fire.

*Luisa answered the door, as the butler was busy, and is quite
sure that it was Miss Harper. She might not have remembered the name, and she had never seen the lady before, but
she is of course knowledgeable about clothes. She said that,
although Miss Harper was not attractive or memorable in
her person, she wore the most remarkable jacket that she,*

Luisa, had ever seen. It was of scarlet silk, she said, and oddly made—loosely fitting, more like a dressing sacque. It was embroidered all over in brilliant colors, with a pattern of animals of some kind. Luisa had never seen such animals, but neither had she ever seen such fine embroidery. Also, Luisa said, Miss Harper wore no hat(!), but only a carved ivory hair ornament. Luisa was quite sad, she said, when she learned that Miss Harper was wearing the jacket when she was found, because, she said, both it and the delicate hair ornament were undoubtedly ruined!!!

Hilda was inclined to agree with Freya's exclamation points. Luisa's concern for the jacket showed a distinct callousness. And if Miss Harper had gone out without a hat, just a comb or whatever it was in her hair, it was a shocking impropriety. However, none of this was to the point at the moment. She read on, with difficulty. The handwriting was becoming even smaller as Freya ran out of paper.

I was not able to learn what aunt and niece discussed, as Luisa was working elsewhere in the house and did not hear. However, as Miss Harper was leaving the house, she made one remark to Luisa which I pass on to you, as it may be enlightening. Luisa said Miss Harper came out of the drawing room looking very sad. Mrs. Stone did not accompany her. Miss Harper asked for her jacket, and as she put it on, said, "Do you have any family, my dear?" Luisa said no, that she had been orphaned at an early age. "Then you may count your blessings. Families are the source of most of the grief in this world." And with that Miss Harper left the house.

That was the extent of the note. Freya had scrawled her name in large letters across the entire back of the sheet, as there was no room at all at the bottom. Hilda eyed the missive with mixed feelings. On the one hand, Freya had provided much food for thought. On the other, she had wasted a great deal of space on nonessentials and failed to mention such important details as the times Miss Harper had arrived and departed, and which direction she had gone when she left.

A sudden gust of chilly wind came through the window, billowing out the curtains and snuffing out the candle flame. In the dark, Hilda suddenly felt her weariness. She had risen very early and worked very late, and had had almost no rest in between. She undressed hastily and went to bed, and no uneasiness about murderers was enough to keep her from solid sleep.

THE WIND ROSE steadily, and the rain came, gently at first and then in a steady torrent. Outside on the lawn the trees tossed and bent. A few early roses shattered under the force of the hard-driving rain; the late lilacs, heavy with fading bloom, drooped their sodden heads nearly to the ground. Hilda slept, oblivious to the wet curtains slapping against the walls, or the pools of rainwater growing steadily on the floor beneath the windowsills.

Across the lawns in the Harper house a lamp burned all night in an upstairs window, where a sleepless watcher gazed intently out into the night.

THE CHILL OF the room finally overbalanced Hilda's need for sleep. She had curled herself into a tighter and tighter ball, but once past her first sleep, she was no longer able to dream herself warm. When she slipped out of bed with a groan to get the blanket, her feet encountered a cold puddle of rain and she was shocked into full wakefulness.

And with wakefulness came awful awareness.

Freya was in terrible danger.

How could she have overlooked so obvious a fact, even for a few hours? Everything was different, was much, much worse, now that Wanda was dead. She, herself, had been afraid to venture down the front drive. She had done it, but she had been afraid. She would infinitely have preferred to stay securely in the great mansion, which might limit her freedom but which would nevertheless protect her from harm.

Freya did not have the option of staying where she was safe. She did not live in her employer's house. Every day she had to leave the tiny house near the *kyrka* that she shared with her brother and sister, and walk nearly two miles to her job, and at the end of her day, often well after nightfall, walk home again. It was not at any time a very pleasant walk, past block after block of the hulking sheds where the Studebakers aged the lumber for their carriages and wagons, over many sets of railroad tracks, down dark streets. Freya had often complained that the walk home, especially, was frightening.

Now that someone was out there killing people who knew about the Harpers, it could be deadly.

Hilda knew that she was prone to act first and think later. But how could she have done anything so abyssmally stupid as this? If anything about the situation was clear, it was that the Harper household was the center of a maelstrom. And by asking Freya to look into Miss Harper's activities, she, Hilda, had pushed her cherished younger sister straight into that violent whirlpool.

It was still raining hard, and the sky was dark, but Hilda knew that morning must be near. By staring hard at the faintly glowing hands of her alarm clock, she made out that they stood at nearly ten past five. She would have to be up and about in a few minutes; there was no time to be lost. She pulled on her dressing gown and thrust her feet into shabby felt slippers. They were nearly worn out anyway, and very likely the rain would ruin them completely, but she dared not get her boots wet, or her uniform; someone might notice and ask why she had been outside so early.

Running silently down the stairs, she made a quick detour into Mr. Clem's study to filch a piece of paper and scribble a quick note in Swedish: *Freya. IMPORTANT! Say NOTHING more to ANYONE about Miss Harper. I will explain when I see you. Hilda.*

Then out the kitchen window and down the drive she flew, with never a thought either to the noise she was making or the pelting rain that was soaking her to the skin. She thrust the folded paper under the rock, hoping it wouldn't be past reading by the time Freya saw it. At least, Hilda thought, she'd had the sense to write it in pencil, so the words wouldn't be washed away.

Precious minutes were lost in the kitchen, cleaning away muddy evidence. She buried her slippers at the bottom of the rubbish barrel, dried her feet, and shivered into her cold bedroom just as the alarm clock went off next door in Norah's room.

Hilda spent most of that terrible morning on two separate levels of existence. With some top layer of her mind, she took care to arrange her wet dressing gown and nightdress in her closet so that no one would notice. She mopped up the rainwater on the floor, spoke courteously to Norah, went about her duties, ate her breakfast. She appeared to listen as Mr. Williams made a solemn little speech about the terrible death of the maid next door and cautioned all the servants to be extra careful. She was faintly aware that he had not forbidden them to go out.

But all of her real attention, as she dusted and scrubbed and polished, was focused on her inner struggle.

What was she to do?

Two people had been murdered. Two! In all her sixteen years of growing up in Sweden she had never known of a single murder.

There had been one killing, when she was about twelve. In the cold and dark of one long snowbound January, a farm laborer had gotten drunk in the village tavern one night, gone berserk, and hit one of the other men over the head with a bottle. He had hanged for it, but no one considered it to be real murder. A man gets winter crazy, drinks too much, and—well, these things happen.

But this! Deliberate, cold-blooded murder, not once but twice. And no one knew who was to blame, but she was sure she knew where to look, and the thought terrified her.

She shuddered, hard. She happened to be in the kitchen at the moment, and Mrs. Sullivan, in a very bad temper over a curdled sauce, snapped, "If you're goin' to get sick, girl, you'll not do it in *my* kitchen. I'd thank you to get whatever you come for and get out of my way!"

Startled out of her reverie, Hilda couldn't remember what she had come for. She murmured some sort of apology and drifted out of the kitchen and back into her thoughts.

There was danger in the air. Danger so sharp she could smell it, taste it sour in her throat. Danger to herself, to others, to the whole community, until this killer was caught.

But who was to catch him? The police were hard on the heels of poor Mr. Kee. He was the convenient villain. He was not a respectable citizen, a powerful political figure. Hilda hoped he was well away from South Bend by now, but if he wasn't, he would find it hard to hide. A Chinese, he could not blend in with others. Perhaps if he went to Chicago there was some hope for him. Hilda had heard that there was a large Chinese community there. She hoped he knew that, too. Because if he didn't, either the police or the frightened, angry mob would find him. And if the mob did, there would be another killing, a lynching.

Of an innocent man.

Or else the police, and the mob, would abandon Kee Long as a bad job and look elsewhere for a murderer. And would they focus on the Harpers? Oh, no! There were attractive scapegoats, and not very far away . . . across the lawn . . .

Hilda shuddered again. Someone had to find the real killer. Someone had to save Mr. Kee. Someone had to make South Bend safe to live in again.

Who?

Am I my brother's keeper?

"All right!" Norah stood in front of Hilda, her arms planted firmly on her hips. "That's three times I've asked ye to set out the glasses. Are ye deaf, or have ye gone looney?"

"I—oh, Norah." She blinked and shook her head.

"And who did ye think it was, Queen Victoria?"

"I am sorry. What did you ask me to do?" Hilda moved to step past Norah.

"Now look here, me girl! I'm not budgin' from this spot until ye talk to me proper, as if ye was hearin' what I was sayin' and knowin' what ye was sayin' back. Ye might as well have been one o' them talkin' machines for all the sense ye've been makin' this mornin'. I want to know what's the matter with ye, and I want to know now!"

Danger . . . danger to herself, danger to others . . . danger . . .

"There is not'ing the matter, Norah. I am sorry my mind has been so absent. Did you say glasses?"

Norah dropped her bullying manner and put her hand on Hilda's arm. "Hilda. Don't ye shut me out, now! I thought we were friends, us two. Won't ye tell me?"

Something in her voice made Hilda's eyes sting. "Yes, we are friends, Norah. That is why I cannot—"

She put a hand to her mouth, but it was too late.

Norah pounced. "So there *is* somethin'. Why can't ye tell me?"

Nothing would quiet her but the truth. "Because I do not want you to be hurt, and it could hurt you to know what worries me."

"I think I'm the best judge o' that."

The two girls stood there in the dining room, motionless. Wide blue eyes locked with sparkling black ones.

In the end it was the blue eyes that blinked and looked away.

"I am afraid, Norah, and I do not know what to do."

In a low voice, she told Norah of her fears for Kee Long, for herself, for her family. She told of Wanda's death, and its terrors. Finally, lowering her voice still further and glancing nervously around the room, she told of her conviction that someone very close to Miss Harper was the murderer.

Norah listened, saying not a word, her eyes growing wider and wider. When Hilda had finished, Norah let out her breath in a soundless whistle.

"I should not have told you," Hilda said dismally. "It would have been better for you not to know." She wiped away the tears that had flowed without her noticing.

"Now don't ye start in on that again. Go and wash yer face and hands. Ye look a sight. And then come back and help me with this dratted table, and we'll decide what to do."

Hilda didn't even notice the "we" as she went to do as she was told.

When she came back, Norah was moving at lightning speed around the table.

"We're behind-time, girl. Get the glasses and set them out, and then fold the napkins. Ye're the best at that. I've decided ye have to do it."

"Have to fold the napkins? Of course, I—"

"May the good Lord and all the saints have mercy! No— have to find out who the murderer is!"

But screw your courage to the sticking-place, And we'll not fail.
—William Shakespeare,
MacBeth, 1606

Hilda studied Norah's face for a full minute, took a deep breath, and released it. "And how will I do that, and still protect my family, and you, and—"

Norah dropped the forks she was setting out and put her hands over her ears. "Hilda Johansson, sometimes I think I'd like to turn ye over me knee, with yer Swedish caution! Do ye think ye're gonna get in front o' them pearly gates some day an' tell St. Peter ye got there by not takin' risks? *Life* is a risk. We all of us risked everything we had, yer family and mine, and all of us immigrants, when we got on them disgustin' boats to come over here—and a lot of us died on those boats, too. Have ye forgotten why we came?"

Hilda opened her mouth to reply, but Norah forestalled her.

"I'll tell ye why, and it wasn't so we could sleep safe in our beds. That we could do at home—if we didn't starve first. We came because there was a chance here for people like us, a chance to make money enough to live, and better than that, too. The freedom maybe to own some land someday, to have nice things, to see our children doin' better than us. And do ye think we could do those things, any of us, without takin' risks? Ye make me tired, me girl, talkin' o' protectin' us. Did any of us ask to be protected?"

"Bravo, Norah," said a quiet voice behind the girls. They whirled, to see Colonel George, one hand resting on the mahogany of the doorway.

"That," he went on, "is as fine a speech as I've ever heard about the spirit that built America. A better speech, I dare say, than any we'll hear tomorrow. Like many of your countrymen, you have a natural gift for eloquence, Norah."

Norah's face was fiery red. "Oh, no, sir," she muttered. "Yer pardon, sir, I should've been doin' me work. Yer lunch'll be late."

He looked at the two girls, smiled a little, and shook his head. "One day, Norah, your children, or your children's children, will be judges in this land, you mark my words. Don't worry about lunch; I'll tell Mother I interrupted your work."

They curtsied to his back. Hilda nodded gravely to Norah. "You are right. I lack courage."

"No, ye don't. What ye lack, me girl, is enough sense of adventure. But we'll teach ye yet, cousin Patrick and I. The Irish may not have the common sense God gave a mule, but we know how to dream, and we know how to enjoy life, too."

"If," said Hilda, her stubborn Swedish nature reasserting itself, "you live long enough."

She spent the rest of the morning working with the detached efficiency of a machine. The napkins were folded into beautifully peaked caps. The silver and crystal were set out in measured geometric perfection. No guest had reason to complain of her service at luncheon; no soup splashed out of the bowl; no courtesy was omitted. But by the time she had helped clear away the meal and taken a few bites of her own lunch, her plans were made. She excused herself and slipped outside.

It was the kind of May day that can't decide whether to be April or June. Clouds drifted fitfully across a watery sun, a few drops of rain would fall, then the sun would come out to turn the world into a steam bath. It was not raining at the moment that Hilda stepped into the back drive; a rainbow, in fact, was forming low in the northern sky. Hilda took it as a good omen.

She walked over to the carriage house to evaluate her choices. She had no time to inquire after her friends in either neighboring house, an action that was, in any case, risky for many reasons. She would simply have to see whether Kristina or Annie was out of doors and available for a brief chat.

She saw the flutter of cloth in the Reynolds backyard and moved closer. Anyone might be hanging up something to dry, or more likely taking something in before the rains came again.

But it was Kristina, and when Hilda approached, her eyes darted back and forth, and she turned to go in the house.

"Kristina, wait! I must talk to you!" Hilda called softly in Swedish.

"No, I cannot, I must go in, I must work, I—"

"*Wait!*" Hilda had caught up with her, and grasped her arm in a none-too-gentle grip. "You are afraid. I understand. But listen to me for just one minute."

Kristina had little choice until Hilda chose to loose her arm, but she was ready to bolt the moment she was free.

"Listen. You have learned something that frightens you, *ja?*" She went on rapidly, without giving Kristina a chance to reply.

"Or perhaps you are frightened because women have been killed, and you do not want to be the next one. I, too, am frightened. I, too, believe that it is not good for a person to know too much about what has happened.

"But do you not see, if you tell me what you know, then there are two of us. If I tell others, there are more. And when there are many people, who all know many things, the killer cannot strike at us all. I have heard a thing that they say in English." She switched to that language. " 'There is safety in numbers.' I think that is very true.

"So I wish you to tell me what you have learned, and I wish you to tell it in English. Loudly. And then, if"—she glanced around her, a little nervously, and continued with a certain bravado—"if someone listens, they will know that I know, as well, and perhaps others, if they have heard. This I think is sense."

Kristina considered for a moment before speaking quietly and in Swedish. "But it will mean that you are in more danger than before. Because you will learn things from many people, and if you can put them together . . ." Her look was shrewd.

Hilda nodded, her characteristic sharp little nod. "That is true, *ja*. But one must take risks to do what is right."

Hilda wished she could sound as sure of her argument as Norah had, but Kristina was apparently convinced. She sighed with relief.

"I know only a little, but I have worried. Now I will tell you, and worry only about you."

She raised her voice only a trifle. The butler must not hear, even for the sake of guaranteeing her safety. There was more than one kind of risk.

"You asked where Miss Harper went on the day of her death," she said in her accented English. "I do not know where she went besides, but I know that she came here, to call on her niece."

"Why did you not tell me when I asked before?" said Hilda angrily.

Kristina was affronted. "It is not my business to talk about the family. I had to think it out. And if you will lose your temper at the first word I speak, I will not tell you the rest."

Hilda bit her tongue. "I am sorry, Kristina. I will not lose my temper. What is the rest?"

Kristina moved closer to the door, her face sulky.

"Please, Kristina! It is important."

"Oh, very well, but I would not do this for many people. I know what they talked about."

Hilda drew in her breath. Here was real news! "What?"

"It was about her will—Miss Harper's will."

Money! Hilda knew little about murder, but she knew that some people would do anything for money. Especially rich people, who seemed, in her limited experience, never to be rich enough, but always to want more, and more. The poor, who expected nothing from life, were grateful for a little. The rich often seemed unhappy even with much. Hilda did not understand, but she knew that it was so.

"What did she say about her will? Did she plan to change it?"

"I do not know," confessed Kristina. "They talk together in the drawing room while I clean the dining room next door. They do not close the door, so I can hear easily. But they speak very fast, and my English is not so good, *ja?* I do not think I hear the word 'change,' but I am not certain."

"Did they argue?"

"*Va' sa du?*"

"Argue. *Bråka.* Become angry. Shout, talk with the hands."

"Oh, yes! At least—Mrs. Reynolds becomes very angry. Miss Harper does not. She is sad and very gentle, and she cries."

"Did she stay long?"

"A few minutes only. Ten, fifteen perhaps. Then she kisses Mrs. Reynolds good-bye, and she goes."

"Did she say anything to you?"

"To me? A grand lady would not talk to me. She say, 'T'ank you,' when I give her the beautiful red jacket. That is all."

"When?"

Kristina looked puzzled.

Barely containing her impatience, Hilda said, "When did Miss Harper visit? When on the clock?"

"Oh. The morning, after breakfast, I do not remember exactly. I must work now."

Hilda could extract no more useful information, and, in any case, she had to get back to her own work. But the cold fear at the back of her mind was growing more insistent.

It could probably be shown by facts and figures that there is no distinctly native American criminal class except Congress.

—Mark Twain, *Following the Equator*, 1897

She knew now what she had to ask Annie, but how to do it subtly was another matter. Perhaps Annie would be inside and she would have no opportunity to ask, thought the cowardly part of her mind.

But Annie, too, was hanging out laundry. That meant, Hilda thought dolefully, that she would be in a bad mood. Perhaps she should turn back, after all?

But she was given no opportunity.

"You! Hilda! Come over here!"

Yes, a truly terrible mood. Hilda's own temper began to get the better of her. She walked a step or two nearer the gate, so she wouldn't have to shout, and then stood rock still.

"It is my rest time, and the house is full of guests; I need my rest. What is it?"

"Oh, la-di-da! Get to rest, do you? It's all very nice for some of us, isn't it? Work in a fine house, get to carry on with a handsome fireman—"

"Annie, do you have something to say to me? Because I do not wish to listen to your complaints. I work just as hard as you."

"Yes, I got somethin' to say, Your Highness! An' that is, you can do your own snoopin' from now on! I dunno where Miss Harper went the day she died, and I don't care. I got my work to do, an' Mrs. Judge, she's jumpy as a cat, pickin' on every move I make, an' the judge, he's lookin' worse 'n' worse, an'—"

"The judge? He is ill?" All Hilda's senses came to the alert.

"Looks like he's about to keel over, if you ask me."

"But you are hardly qualified to give an opinion, are you?"

The voice was male, and cold. James had come across the grass so quietly that neither woman had noticed his approach. Hilda jumped; Annie clutched at her breast.

"Lor', Mr. James, you scared the livin' daylights out of me!"

"A pity you didn't bite your tongue, isn't it?" he said nastily. "You'd better learn to hold that tongue, or somebody'll cut it out for you."

Annie stood with her mouth open.

"Oh, don't look so stupid! I will not have you gossiping about my father or any other member of this family. Surely even you can understand that."

It was the first time Hilda had seen Mr. James even close to sober. She thought now that she preferred him drunk. She was not feeling very kindly toward Annie, either, but someone had to take her part.

"Annie is concerned about the judge's health, sir. That is not gossip!"

He rounded on her. "And just who're you, anyway, sticking your oar in?" He looked at her more closely and put a hand on her arm. "Hmm. If you're a new maid, my mother's showing better taste than she usually does. You're pretty good-looking."

Hilda tried to back away. "My name is Hilda, sir. I am house-maid to Mrs. Studebaker. Excuse me, sir, I must—"

"James! What are you doing? Why are you not at the office?"

Mrs. Harper approached them at a near run. Her blotchy face and red eyes looked, to Hilda, as though she had been crying. Certainly her hair was unkempt and her costume careless in the extreme; it was not even entirely black.

James dropped Hilda's arm. She rubbed it furtively; there would be bruises where his fingers had bitten in at the sound of his mother's voice.

"What are you doing?" Mrs. Harper repeated, her voice high and shrill. "You ought to be working."

"I came home for a moment," he said shortly. "As you see."

"Why?"

"To get some papers I needed, if you must know."

"What papers? What for?"

"Even if you could understand, which I doubt, as you have no legal training, I prefer not to discuss the firm's business with anyone, particularly not in front of the servants." He strode back to the house without another word.

"Well!" said Annie. "I never heard Mr. James talk to you that way, an' certain sure he done never spoke to *me* that way in all my days, an' if he ever does again, I'll—"

"You'll keep your peace, Annie," said Mrs. Harper. "And you," she said, turning to Hilda, "do you have a message for me from Mrs. Studebaker?"

"No, madam."

"Then what are you doing here?"

"I was speaking to Annie; I—"

"You have no business interrupting Annie's work, not to mention neglecting your own. I shall speak to Mrs. Studebaker about it. Go away."

Hilda had to clench her teeth so hard to keep from answering that they hurt all the way back to the house.

Her anger sustained her through the next hour of work, until at last she could plod up the three flights of service stairs. Once she reached her room, however, her energy deserted her. She removed her boots and dropped onto her bed with a heavy sigh, not even bothering to undress.

Her body was crying out for rest, and she needed her sleep. As hard as she worked, she deserved her sleep. She punched her pillow into a more comfortable shape, and tried to empty her mind.

It was no use. Her restless thoughts refused to be banished. Wearily she sat up. If she could not rest, she could at least try to bring order to her mind.

What did she know?

Little enough, in all truth. She knew that Miss Harper had visited her two nieces the day she died. She did not know when she had seen Mrs. Stone, but Kristina had said she had visited Mrs. Reynolds "after breakfast." Soon after breakfast, probably, if Kristina was still cleaning the dining room. So it made sense to suppose that Miss Harper had gone straight from the judge's house to see Mrs. Reynolds, and from there to Mrs. Stone's.

What else?

She had talked about her will to Mrs. Reynolds, and it had been a brief but stormy discussion. Had she had the same talk with Mrs. Stone? Again, there was no way to know, but whatever they had talked about, it had upset Miss Harper, if the information Freya had gleaned from the maid Luisa was to be believed.

And the judge looked so ill Annie was afraid he "might keel over."

Hilda sighed deeply. The conclusion was inescapable. The judge had sacrificed a great deal to follow his political career. He was plainly in need of money. If his sister had money to leave, he might reasonably suppose that she would leave at least part of it to him. But perhaps she had talked about changing her will. The judge would have tried to persuade her not to do so; the conversation had gone wrong; the judge had reached out . . .

Hilda put her hands over her eyes, but the vision in her mind could not be shut out. She slid down in bed again and pulled the pillow over her head.

What would happen to someone who accused Judge Harper of murder?

Proudly, sadly and with unelastic step the thinned guard of the civil war tramped up Washington street yesterday afternoon to do honor to its legions fallen in battle.

South Bend *Tribune*,

May 31, 1900

ecoration Day, 1900, dawned with an uncertain sky hanging low above the city. Hilda was sure it would rain, which would not only spoil the parade but impede her plans. She went about her work with one eye on the weather, but the sky cleared by noon, and she began to feel apprehension only about whether it would work, what she had decided to do.

Washington Street was bright with flags and patriotic banners. Children, freed from their classrooms for the day, ran excitedly up and down the street, eager for the parade to get under way.

Hilda loved parades. She especially loved marches like the

ones the St. Hedwige Cornet Band was going to play today. And Patrick, her own Patrick, would be out there marching with the fire department, in his best uniform with brass buttons shining.

It was a shame she was going to miss it all.

The family and their guests had gone off to a pre-parade picnic at the spacious country house of Mr. Clem's brother, J.M., so most of the servants' duties were completed early. They ate their own cold lunch in excited haste, cleaned up with more speed than care, and went off to enjoy the holiday.

Hilda went off to become a burglar.

She had worried all evening, and tossed and turned half the night, but by morning a plan was fixed in her head. She wasn't sure she hadn't dreamed it, and she was definitely unsure whether or not it was a good idea, but she was going to do it.

She was going to steal Miss Harper's will.

It was a desperate measure, but the only thing she could think to do. No excuse she could make would convince a lawyer that she needed to see it. She dared not go to the police with her idea; they would not believe her without proof, and she hoped, in any case, that they had forgotten her existence.

No, the only thing to do was to go to the Harper law offices, find the will, and read it—steal it if necessary. And the best time to do so, the time when surely no one would be there, was during the Decoration Day parade.

She had enlisted Norah's aid, though not without a long and bitter argument.

"Ye're daft, that's what! Ye'll be caught, ye know, and thrown in jail, and none of us will ever see ye again, not me, nor Patrick, nor yer sisters—never look on those bright eyes again, that golden hair—"

"Norah, stop!" She dammed the flow of Irish eloquence. "You talk like Patrick. It sounds well, but it means nothing. I will not be caught. All that is for you to do is to say I am with my family, if anyone asks. You will do that for me, *ja?*"

"And send ye to yer death?"

But even the poetic Irish imagination was no match, in the end, for stubborn Swedish determination. Much against her will, and with dire imprecations, Norah promised to tell no one what Hilda was really doing, unless she did not return within a reasonable time.

"When the parade is over, and they have all returned from the cemetery," said Hilda firmly. "Not until then may you say a word to anyone."

"Not even Patrick?"

"Especially not Patrick! He would try to stop me."

"For all the good it would do him," Norah muttered, but she agreed.

Hilda waited until the first unit of the parade, the platoon of metropolitan police, were visible down at the corner of Michigan Street, where the line of march began. Then she melted out of the crowd gathered on the lawn of Tippecanoe Place, and made her way to the law offices of Harper, Hill, Brookins, and Harper.

There were only a few blocks to go, but she had to walk by way of the back streets, which took her a little longer. The offices were straight up Washington, in the first block west of Michigan—the very center of town, and the very place where the parade mustered. She would be too conspicuous walking through those crowds. So she walked up Jefferson instead, a quiet residential street, deserted on this festive day.

At one corner she looked up the side street and saw a fire truck passing, its high-stepping horses beautifully groomed, its red paint and brass fittings gleaming brightly. She sighed at what she was missing, but persevered. Waiting until the cornet band was playing a loud Sousa march, she slipped up the alley between Main and Michigan streets to the back door of the office building.

It was a plain building, built of wood and housing a drugstore on the ground floor. There were far finer offices on the street, those of George Ford, for example, and the Odd Fellows Block, just a few doors away. The Harpers, however, had always been here, before they had become one of the leading firms in town, and it was likely they would stay here until the building burned down. Which, Hilda thought with a shudder as she climbed the rickety outside stairs up the back of the building, it was very likely to do some day. These old buildings went up like tinder, despite the best efforts of Patrick and his colleagues. Even the standpipe, the pride of South Bend's fire-fighting system, usually couldn't supply water to the hydrants fast enough to stop the flames.

The Harpers, however, clung to the old building. Their firm had too sound a reputation to require fancy trappings.

They also, Hilda discovered with great relief when she got to the top of the stairs, apparently had a careless staff. A tall, broad window on the landing had been left open a crack. It was the work of a moment to raise the wide sash still farther and climb inside.

Hilda found herself in a dusty storeroom full of large filing boxes. Her heart sank as she looked at them. There must have been over a hundred boxes, all neatly labeled, in stacks reaching to the ceiling. If she had to go through all these, she would be here till the middle of next week. Except that she wouldn't; she'd have been discovered and hauled away.

. . .thrown in jail, and none of us will ever see ye again . . .

Then the moment of panic passed and her common sense reasserted itself. These boxes were covered with dust. They were plainly old files of inactive matters, probably left undisturbed from one year to the next. Miss Harper had died a week ago. Her will would be set out on someone's desk or in an active file.

Outside, the trumpet band was long gone. Drums, ever nearer, beat a muffled cadence, and Hilda knew that the Civil War veterans who were bringing up the rear of the parade were not far away. They would march all the way to the cemetery. Schoolgirls along the parade route would give them flowers to place, reverently, on the graves of their fellow soldiers who had fallen in battle. Then, after solemn speeches, the whole procession would re-form and march back. But people didn't always stay to watch their return. She didn't have time to waste.

She eased herself out of the storeroom very quietly. No one was in the building, of course, but just in case . . . Once in the tiny hallway, she saw four doors, two on either side of the hall, with a staircase at the far end. The four offices would belong to the three partners (only one of whom, Mr. James, was still a Harper) and the secretary. Well, the secretary probably wouldn't have the will. She was betting on Mr. James, whose name was lettered in bright, new-looking gold on the frosted glass of the nearest door. She reached for the knob.

The door was locked.

That stopped her for a moment, but there was more than one way to skin a cat. The door with "Harper, Hill, Brookins, and Harper" lettered on it in older, duller gold was next to James Harper's. That was plainly the secretary's office, and there was probably a door leading from it into the lawyer's office.

The secretary's door was also locked.

Hilda stamped her foot in frustration, and shook the doorknob, hard. Nothing whatever happened, except that the glass rattled alarmingly. Hilda took her hand off the brass handle as if it had suddenly turned hot. It would never do to break the glass.

But how, how, how was she to get in?

She stooped and squinted into the keyhole with but little

hope. The door would have been locked from the outside, and the key taken away.

She eyed the transom, far up at the top of the high door. It was open, and there had, she remembered, been a stepladder in the storage room, probably to get at the tops of those tall stacks of boxes. Oh, yes, she might be able to climb in over the transom. But what would she do on the other side, fall to the floor? And how would she get out again?

In the street outside, the drums had passed and receded. Time was waning, and Hilda was no nearer her goal.

In sudden desperation she pulled off her hat, set it on the floor, and removed one of the strong hairpins that were meant to hold her fine gold braids atop her head. One braid immediately flopped down. She ignored it, but bent intently to try her hand at lock-picking.

She knew very little of locks, but she had heard that it was possible to open them without a key. She poked around with the pin, trying frantically to damp her emotions and marshal her thoughts into a helpful, logical pattern.

One turned a key so that the notches in it were pointed upward. That must mean that the working part of the lock was above the keyhole. Sure enough, the probing hairpin encountered irregularities at the top of the hole. It barely touched them, however; clearly the pin was the wrong shape.

Hilda removed it, straightened it out, bent one end upward, and tried again.

This time she was rewarded. Something moved; the hairpin felt the resistance of a spring. Holding the pin in place with one hand, Hilda tried the doorknob.

Nothing.

Well, maybe there was more than one of these spring things. She wished she could see inside the lock, but one might as well wish for the moon. Removing another hairpin and modifying it, she tried with both hands, and was eventually able to move another whatever-it-was. But that left her with no hand to turn the knob, and the moment she released the pressure on the hairpins, the pieces of the mechanism dropped back into place.

She could easily have become discouraged, but she could taste success now, and her stubborn resolve would not allow her to quit.

What was needed was something to hold things in place as she was able to move them, until she could move them all—surely there couldn't be more than three or four of the dratted things in so small a space. The hairpins were too slippery, too round and thin. Something flat was needed. Flat, but very narrow, like a boning knife at its business end, or—

With admirable speed, as the thought struck her, she unbuttoned her shirtwaist, took it off, and removed one of the steel stays of her corset.

It worked like a charm. She was gaining expertise, and it took only a little time to move the first two pieces of the lock and hold them in place with the corset stay. She took a deep breath, wiggled a hairpin farther back, and moved it, feeling something move, lift—

With a lovely rattle, something fell and slid aside. She loosed her hold on her unorthodox keys, wiped her slippery hands on her skirt, and tried the door.

The bolt rattled loosely. It had moved, but not quite enough. Hilda uttered a Swedish word she had heard only once before—from her brother, that time he'd smashed his thumb with the hammer—and pulled the long pin from her hat.

That hat pin was her most prized possession, a gift from Gudrun for Hilda's eighteenth birthday. It was real gold—well, gold plate, anyway—and if the white stones studding it weren't diamonds, they were Sears Roebuck's best imitation.

Without a single thought to its value, Hilda thrust the pin into the oak of the door frame, viciously shoved it aside to bend a hook into the end of the tough wire, jerked it out, and jimmied the bolt. It moved sweetly aside with a little *snick*, her improvised tools fell out of the lock, and the office was at her disposal.

And after all this, she muttered to herself as she replaced her discarded items of clothing, I had better be able to get into Mr. James's office, and the will had better be there!

It was. It was sitting on the middle of his cluttered desk, an impressive document written in an impressive Spencerian hand that Hilda was going to find very hard to read, but the heading, "Last Will and Testament of Mary Harper," was quite plain.

Hilda sank to the office chair. Now that the prize was hers, she was weak in the knees. Her hair was coming down. Her hat, without its pin, wouldn't stay on her head. Both her hat and her waist, a plain but good one, were streaked with dust from the floor where she had dropped them, and both were damp with nervous sweat.

She didn't have time, however, to worry about her appearance. Already she could hear the distant strains of martial music. The parade was coming back! Hurriedly she bent her head to the will and tried to decipher the difficult writing and the unfamiliar legal language.

A frown grew on her face. What she thought she was reading made no sense at all. She shook her head, turned back to the first page, and looked at the date. Maybe this was a draft of the new will, the one Miss Harper had intended to sign the day she died?

No, it was dated in July of 1890, and—she flipped to the end—was signed and witnessed.

Then why, with the exception of small bequests to the three Harper children, did the will leave all of Miss Harper's worldly possessions to the First Methodist Episcopal Church?

Hilda had misread it. That had to be the trouble. Doggedly she went back, reading one word at a time, pronouncing them aloud . . .

The drums roused her. Oh, *Herre Gud*, the drums! They marked the end of the parade! They would be coming back at any moment, and someone might come to the office . . .

She rolled the will into a tight cylinder, thrust it in her pocket, and ran out through the secretary's office. There was no time to think about locking the door with her clumsy lock picks. She found the storeroom, knocked over a box, replaced it in nervous haste, and in doing so jarred open the door to a small, shallow cupboard hanging on the wall.

It was a key box. There, clearly labeled, were the keys to the entire office, hanging neatly on hooks.

She took the one she needed, ran back with it and locked the door, and regained the storeroom just as someone opened the front door and started up the stairs.

Hilda discovered a whole vocabulary she hadn't known she possessed as she squeezed out through the window and down the stairs.

It is a capital mistake to theorize before one has data.

—Arthur Conan Doyle,
"A Scandal in Bohemia," 1892

Patrick was sunk in gloom.

"Ye've been and gone and done it now, me girl," he said, shaking his head dolefully. "And for what, now tell me that? You're no better off than ye were, and you'll be clapped in jail if anyone finds out."

"No one will know. If no one tells," Hilda added pointedly. "He is not a neat person. Papers were everywhere. He will think that he mislaid it, and he will look, and accuse his secretary, and they will not know it is gone until some days have passed, and in the meanwhile I will put it back. Now that I know how to pick a lock," she added smugly, and picked up a chicken leg.

Patrick put down his buttered roll. "You're never goin' back there?" His voice rose in outrage.

"You are shouting, Patrick," replied Hilda through a mouthful of chicken. "People will hear. The deviled eggs are very good; you should taste one."

It was late afternoon. They were picnicking in Howard Park, feasting on the basket of food Hilda had packed. Mrs. Sullivan might have a terrible temper at times, but she was a marvelous cook, and generous with special-occasion food for the servants. Hilda, having returned home, stowed the will safely away, and repaired the damage to her toilette, was now looking, and feeling, very cool and sure of herself. She did not, however, want everyone else in the park to know what they were talking about.

Patrick lowered his voice, but it was still full of wrath. He had intended to enjoy himself on this picnic. He had a brand-new—well, almost brand-new—pair of knickerbockers in a dashing brown-and-green check, and a new ribbon on his hat. And Hilda had gone and spoiled everything with these shenanigans.

"I brought one of me mother's glasses. I thought we'd take it to the lady who gave you the lemonade, after we ate." He sounded sulky.

"But we can still do that, Patrick! It is good of you to remember. And I do not go to return the will until night, of course."

"Night! You're goin' there at night? And aren't you the one who keeps goin' around sayin' how much danger there is, and how the police are goin' to get ye if the murderer doesn't first? Oh, Norah's told me how scairt ye've been."

Hilda's expression boded no good for Norah. "There is no reason to fear going back to the office. No one will see, and you, Patrick, if you are fearful, you will go with me."

"Not tonight, I won't," he replied sourly, "nor the next, nor the next. I'm on duty, nights, for the rest of the week."

"Oh." She didn't actually want to go back to that office by herself. Nor did she want to admit that to Patrick. "Well, then, I will take Norah. She will stand and watch for me."

"I give up," said Patrick with a groan. "You're the most inconsistent girl I ever met."

"I am not. I wish to protect myself. The way to do that is to put the will back."

"So you say. And I want to know what you think you've accomplished by stealin' it in the first place."

"But I have accomplished much! I know, now, that I have been wrong. The judge did not kill Miss Harper for her money."

"And I suppose you know now who did kill her?" said Patrick sarcastically.

"But of course! It was the judge."

"You just *said*—," Patrick roared.

"Keep your *voice* down! I said he did not do it for money. He did it for some other reason. I do not know what. *No*, Patrick, do not throw the roll at me. I am serious, now. He killed her, Patrick. I know he did. But why?"

Patrick finished eating the roll, but he remained skeptical. "I don't know how you can be so sure," he complained when he could talk again.

"We have talked of this, Patrick. Part of my reasons you know. But I have not told you—I have not told anyone what I heard at the funeral."

In a whisper, she related Mrs. Harper's words to her husband. " 'No matter what you've done.' Those were her very words. And he looks very ill, worse every day. Patrick, *something* is the matter. What else could it be?"

Patrick was shaken. He mulled over her words while he absentmindedly ate the rest of the deviled eggs, finally hitting on what seemed most important at the moment.

"Why did ye not tell me this before?" he demanded.

Hilda looked at her lap. "I did not like to say it. I did not want to believe it. But—there are too many things, now, for me not to believe, Patrick. Too much—evidence." She brought out the word with some satisfaction. "I am sure that he did it."

Patrick sat back, leaning one elbow on the blanket. "All right. I'm not sayin' you're right, mind you. But for the sake of the argument, suppose you are. How're ye goin' to prove it?"

"I do not know, and I am troubled. Before I can do more, I must know why—and I do not have the idea."

She looked so woebegone that Patrick was moved to pity, an emotion he seldom felt with regard to Hilda.

"Well, then, we'll have to figger it out, won't we? Why do people kill people, besides for money?"

"They go berserk when they are drunk," Hilda offered from the one case in her experience.

"Umm. I can't see the judge going berserk, can you?"

"No. He is too cold and reserved."

"Well, then. Sometimes a man will kill in a fight over a woman, but somehow I don't think . . ."

Hilda almost giggled. "No. I think he cares only a little about women. We do this the wrong way, Patrick. It is not, Why do people kill people? It is, Why would the judge kill someone?"

"The judge is a person, just like anybody else."

She shook her head decidedly. "No. He is not just like anyone else. No one is just like anyone else. Everyone has reasons for what he does, ideas which are important to him, and they are not all the same. The judge is one person only, not 'people,' he is—" Her hands fluttered, reaching for the English word.

"Unique," supplied Patrick.

"Yes! Thank you. So we must think, about what does *he* care enough to kill?"

"Well, let's see. He's a good Methodist."

"Ye-es." Her voice was full of doubt. "He goes to the church, but he does not follow the teachings. He serves wine at his house, and—oh, he is not like Miss Harper, who I think was a truly religious woman. The judge, he goes to church because it is respectable, the way most people do, or perhaps because his wife makes him go. Religion for him is not—not a passion."

"Umm." Patrick relapsed into silence, then sat up with such suddenness that the picnic basket was upset. "Hilda, what fools we've been! Politics, of course!"

"Oh, Patrick, you are right! And you are smart, but if you cannot be quieter, we must leave, and I do not want to leave. It is beautiful here." She looked at him severely while she put the picnic basket to rights. He grinned and put a finger to his lips with exaggerated caution.

Satisfied, Hilda handed Patrick a somewhat squashed piece of chocolate cake and took one herself. "But yes, you are right, and we have been stupid. It is politics that he cares about more than anything. Why, he even said so, the night I had to ladies'-maid the mistresses at his house."

"He said politics were that important?" Patrick wiped crumbs from his mouth.

"He said"—Hilda frowned, trying to remember—"he said that his family had sacrificed for his political career. I could not see his face, of course, but his voice did not sound as if he was very sorry. I think what he meant was that he would do anything, even if it meant hardship, for his career. But why, Patrick, would that lead him to kill?"

"I can't imagine. Unless—" Patrick put his cake on his tin plate. He looked excited, but this time he kept his voice very low indeed.

"Listen, Hilda. I think I've got it. We know the politics in this town aren't always honest. Bribery in the police department—all that. Suppose the judge isn't honest either?"

Hilda was more shocked at the idea of Judge Harper's dishonesty than she had been at the idea of his killing people. "But that would be terrible! A dishonest judge—that is the worst thing—in a democracy . . ." Words failed her.

"And that is just why he might kill to prevent anybody knowing! If he took bribes, say. Or if he were bribing others, for their votes. Or anything like that. And suppose Miss Harper found out."

"She would have told," said Hilda with absolute certainty. "She was a religious woman. She would be sorry to tell about her brother, but—oh! I have remembered something!"

"What? And now you're the one shoutin', me girl."

"Yes. But I remembered what Freya wrote to me in that note. She said that Luisa said—it is complicated, but Miss Harper talked to Luisa as she left, after her visit to Mrs. Stone. And she said that families were a trouble—and she looked very sad, Luisa said! And, oh—Kristina—next door?"

Patrick nodded to show he knew who Kristina was.

"She said Miss Harper cried that morning as she left the house!"

Slowly Patrick nodded. "She had somethin' bad worryin' her, that's certain."

"And I thought she had told them she would change her will, and they—her nieces—had been angry. But if she had told them about their father . . . no!" She shook her head in vexation. "That is not right. She did talk about her will. Kristina heard her say the word."

Patrick finished his cake, thinking deeply. "Your friend Kristina," he said after a pause. "How good is her English?"

"Not as good as mine," Hilda said a little smugly.

"So do you think she could tell the difference between someone talking about her will, and someone saying she 'will' do something?"

"Oh. Oh! Patrick, if we were not here in a park, where people could see, I t'ink I would kiss you!"

"Just my luck," Patrick grumbled, but he couldn't keep the grin from his face.

"She goes there." Hilda was rapt in the reconstruction of the morning Miss Harper died. "She tells Mrs. Reynolds of the judge's wickedness, and says she *will* tell everyone. Mrs. Reynolds is angry, and Miss Harper cries. Then she goes to Mrs. Stone and tells her the same thing, and is again sad. Then—" She came to a halt, and finally finished flatly. "Then I do not know what happens. She goes home—I mean, back to the judge's house. And—and somehow the judge knows, and he kills her, and—"

"Sshh!" Patrick grabbed her arm and pinched it, hard. "Someone's coming!"

A man Hilda had never seen before strode across the grass toward them.

"Oh, it's Joe Luther," said Patrick in surprise. "A fireman. And a good day to ye, Joe," he called out when the man was close enough. "I'd like ye to meet my friend, Miss Johansson."

"Ma'am," said Joe politely, doffing his straw hat. "Patrick. You'll excuse me buttin' in, but there's something"—he looked around quickly, and lowered his voice—"something you need to know."

They both caught his note of urgency. "Sit down, Mr. Luther," said Hilda quickly.

He dropped to the blanket. "Patrick, you've been asking around about that Chinaman, Kee Long?"

There were two gasps. Two pairs of eyes widened; two mouths parted slightly, the better to hear.

"He's been found. He's been hiding out all this time in an empty house, but one of our men caught him trying to steal some food from the garbage, out behind the firehouse. He's at the firehouse now, and he's had a meal, but he won't be safe there for long. I thought you'd want to know, right away!"

We often hear . . . that guilt can look like innocence. I believe it
to be infinitely the truer axiom that innocence can look like guilt.
—Wilkie Collins, *The*
Moonstone, 1868

They repacked the picnic basket with more haste than care.
Only Hilda's anguished cries kept Patrick from throwing
everything on top of the plates.

"Please, Patrick! They are only tin, for picnics, but Mrs.
Sullivan will skin me if you dent them." "Skin me" was her latest
piece of American slang; even in her distraction she was pleased
at remembering it.

On the way to the firehouse they argued furiously, the two
of them. Joe followed and kept a discreet silence.

"But you can't go traipsin' in there! Women aren't allowed
upstairs in the firehouse. And besides, you bein' there would
just call attention to what we want to hide!"

192 | JEANNE M. DAMS

"I will go wit' you! It was I who made you look for the Chinese man. It was I who told you he was in danger. Do you think I will do somet'ing to harm him?"

"It's not practical, I tell you, all of us bargin' in like a herd o' cattle—"

"Patrick." Hilda stopped in the middle of Main Street. It was fortunate that there was little traffic on this holiday afternoon. Her voice, as she went on, was dangerously quiet. "You will not call me a cow, Patrick. And if it is so bad that we all go, you will take the basket back, and I will go by myself. Or," she said, turning and smiling brilliantly at Joe, "or Mr. Luther will escort me. We do not need you."

Joe's warm smile in return quieted Patrick in a hurry. Joe was American born, and Protestant. Patrick did not feel that a friendship between him and Hilda was to be encouraged.

"All right, then," he said sulkily. "But we'd best hurry." He marched across the street with such alacrity that Hilda had to run to keep up with him. Behind Patrick's back, she exchanged a grin with Joe.

No one was smiling, though, when they got to the firehouse. Joe, in a bashful undertone, had managed to persuade Hilda that Patrick's reasoning was sound. "Maybe it'd be better, after all, Miss Johansson," he had whispered, "if you waited in the alley behind the station. We could bring Mr. Kee out, quietlike, for you to talk to. He's awful scared, and I think he might run if there are too many people. This'll be safer for him."

Hilda had said nothing to Patrick, but now as they reached their goal, she dropped back. "Give me the picnic basket," she said, her tone defying Patrick to comment. "I will wait here."

Wisely, he said nothing, but went ahead with Joe, the two of them trying hard to look as though they were on an ordinary errand.

Hilda waited. She paced. She studied the back of the fire-house, which was not very interesting. She listened to the noise of the traffic, which was not very loud. She fretted. Her tempera-ment was made for action, not delay. Would they never come? Had something happened? Maybe Mr. Kee had run away again. Maybe the police had found him!

She had nearly decided to go in and see for herself, regardless of the consequences, when the three of them came out the back door, Patrick and Joe and a short, terrified looking man in a fireman's uniform whose trousers were turned up several times and wrapped round at the waist with rope.

"You were very long!" she whispered furiously.

"Five minutes," said Patrick in surprise.

"It took us a while to talk him into coming out. I know it must have seemed long, with you so worried," said Joe, and Pat-rick glared at the warm, understanding tone.

"I go, yes, please?" said the man in uniform anxiously, and all the attention turned to him.

"Not yet, Mr. Kee. We have to figure out where you'll be safe," said Joe.

"This is Mr. Kee?" asked Hilda. "Why is he dressed that way?"

"It was all we could find in a hurry," said Joe. "He was dressed in his own clothes—a long robe, like a dress, and funny pants. He stuck out like a sore thumb. This way he looks pretty funny, but at least he doesn't look quite so Chinese. And we've tucked his pigtail up in his hat."

Mr. Kee, who had followed only a word or two of Joe's speech, said again, "I go now, yes?"

"Yes," said Hilda with sudden decision. "Mr. Kee, you will come home with me. I will hide you. You will be safe. Safe, do you understand?"

He understood, at least, the compassion in her voice. He turned to her and bowed low, and she caught the glimmer of tears in his eyes. "I go with you, yes. These men"— he bowed to Joe and Patrick— "they are good to me. Feed me, give me clothes. You make me safe, yes?"

"Yes," said Hilda again. "But the uniform will not do, Patrick. He does not look Chinese, but he looks foolish. People will notice. Patrick, you are shorter than Mr. Luther, and you are wearing knickerbockers. You will have to give him your clothes."

His prized new clothes! Patrick opened his mouth to protest, but his eyes lighted on Mr. Kee, looking small, confused, and very forlorn. He sighed.

"The uniform won't fit me, by a long way," was his only comment as he shepherded Mr. Kee back through the door.

When he had changed clothes yet again, Mr. Kee looked— well, still peculiar, Hilda thought, but better, rather like a little boy in his father's clothes. He was shorter than Hilda by several inches, and to further the illusion, she took him firmly by the hand.

"We pretend," she said carefully when Mr. Kee, shocked at the liberty, tried to pull away. "You are my son, yes? I am your mother. We play that this is so. You will carry the basket. It is better."

Resigned, Mr. Kee bowed.

"And you, Patrick, you will take the glass back to the lady, please. It is the house with the green porch, on Water Street, just past St. Joseph's Church. I do not remember the number. It is kind of you to do this for me, Patrick. I have worried about the glass."

She had forgotten it, if truth be told, but she wanted Patrick out of the way without an argument. It would not do to have a procession escorting her and her peculiar-looking "son" back to Tippecanoe Place.

Patrick did argue, of course, especially when Joe Luther courteously offered to accompany Hilda and Mr. Kee, but Hilda got her way, as she usually did, and she and Mr. Kee set off, alone.

The ill-matched couple didn't talk on their way. Mr. Kee was bewildered and unsure of his English, and Hilda was thinking hard. This was a foolish and dangerous task she was undertaking, but from the moment she had seen the frightened little man, she had known she must do something. And there was an excellent hiding place in the big mansion. The greatest risk was going to be smuggling Mr. Kee inside.

Or perhaps the risk was not so great, after all. Hilda squinted at the sun on its downward arc. It must be after six. That meant that the Studebakers and their guests would be upstairs dressing for the gala dinner tonight, and the only servants who didn't have the day off—Anton and Michelle and the visitors' personal maids and footmen—would be attending them. With any luck at all, nobody would be around to see them as they crept into the great house.

"Oh!"

Hilda jumped, startled to hear Mr. Kee speak.

"You live in hotel? Maybe not so good, with people here, there—"

She was leading him up the back drive, and he was pulling back against her firm grip on his hand.

"No, it is not a hotel, only a very big house. A very *fine* house," she added with pride.

"This a house? All this?" His eyes opened very wide, and his tone was respectful as he asked, "You are rich, miss?"

Hilda giggled. "No. I am a servant here. I *work* in this house, *ja*—I mean, yes?"

Mr. Kee looked confused again, but trotted along obediently.

"Now," said Hilda as they approached the bottom of the basement stairs, "you must be very quiet. You will not say anything, and you will come with me. Do you understand what I am saying?"

Mr. Kee's sallow skin was turning even paler with fright, but he bowed. "I no say word. I go with you."

"That is right. And if we see anyone, you will pretend to be a little boy. Yes?"

He bowed again.

Hilda eased the door open, put a finger to her lips, and listened.

The big house was very still. Whatever activity was going on two floors above, there was no sound in the basement. Hilda pulled Mr. Kee through the door, past the kitchen and pantry doors, and down a few steps. She stopped at another door and gestured to Mr. Kee to put the picnic basket on the floor. "Be careful!" she whispered. "There are stairs, and it is dark!"

Stepping with great care, she led Mr. Kee down a few steps. "Close the door behind you!"

Utter darkness. Mr. Kee moaned gently.

"Do not worry. I will get a light, but we must hide you. Come with me. I will not let you fall."

Holding tightly to the rail with one hand and to Mr. Kee with the other, she felt her way to the bottom of the stairs.

"Wait here. Do not move. I will be right back."

"Please, miss—" The voice was weak with fright.

"Do not *worry!*" Hilda was becoming impatient. It wasn't easy to help some people. "All is well. I return with light, in one moment!"

It took more than a moment. Hilda ran up the stairs as fast as she dared, and had barely closed the door behind her when she heard feet on the service stairs. There was no place to hide. She took a deep breath and tried to look as though she had just come out of the kitchen.

"Oh! You startled me!"

It was one of the visiting maids.

"I, too, was startled." You do not know how much, Hilda thought grimly.

"Say, where is the laundry? I need to iron this shawl, but I'm lost. This is sure a big place, huh?"

"It is a very fine house," said Hilda primly. "I show you the laundry, but I do not think there is a fire for the irons. It is damped. Do you have time to build it up and let it get hot?"

"Sure, plenty of time. You're a foreigner, ain't you?"

"I am Swedish, but I have lived in America for three years. Here is the laundry, and here is the stove, and the coal. The irons are here. I am sorry I do not have time to talk. Excuse me."

"Hey, wait a minute, can't you?"

But Hilda had gone. Across the hall to the kitchen, get rid of the picnic basket. Find a candle stub, matches, and an old saucer. Get back to the subbasement door, pray the talkative maid doesn't see through the open laundry door . . .

If she saw, Hilda heard no cry. She closed the door behind her with the least possible noise, lit the candle, and hurried down the stairs.

The terror-stricken Chinese had sunk to the floor beside the stairs, and for a moment Hilda was afraid he had fainted. But the light brightened his spirits. He stood up. "I happy to see you, miss," he said fervently.

"I am sorry I was so long," she whispered. "Come over here."

This part of the subbasement was a veritable labyrinth that served several purposes. The bottom of the elevator shaft was here, as well as several rooms devoted to the storage of seldom used items. There was also a room where odds and ends were kept, the sort of castoffs that accumulate in any house, no matter how grand. Kitchen discards lived here, pots with holes that would one day— perhaps—be mended, old china, tea towels that were past their prime. There were toys that Master George had played with before he grew big and went off to school, and, most important for Hilda's purposes, there was furniture—a few kitchen chairs, a table or two, and an old cast-iron bed from one of the servants' rooms. It had lost one of its legs, but it could be propped up, and it would make a comfortable little nest for Mr. Kee.

Hilda set the candle carefully on one of the tables and sat, gesturing to Mr. Kee to do the same.

"You will be safe here," she whispered. "You will have to be quiet, in case anyone upstairs might hear you, but no one will come down here. No one except me. I will come to bring you food. Do you understand?" She looked at him doubtfully. To one accustomed to the mobile Western countenance, his face seemed impassive, inexpressive.

But he smiled and nodded, several times. "It is good place, miss."

Hilda looked a little dubious. "Well—it is cluttered, but it is clean." She took a deep breath. "Now this you will not like, but I must take the candle away."

This time the inscrutable face did show some emotion.

"Yes, it is not good, but the first rule in this house is that we may use no candles. The house has much wood, you understand. It might burn." She decided not to tell him that it had, once. He was frightened enough already.

"You will not have to remain here long. I have the idea. Do you know the city Chicago?"

He frowned. "No, miss."

"It is a very big city, not a long way from here by train. Many Chinese people live there, and they will be kind to you." She had no idea whether they would or not, really, but surely they would look after their own. "Do you have money?"

Mr. Kee looked sad. She was beginning to be able to read

his face. "No money, miss. Nothing. Left all at big school, with good fathers."

"Ah. Well, do not worry. I will find money for you, and think of a way to get you to the train. But for now, you are safe here. Are you hungry?"

"Yes, miss. They give me food, the other men, but not so much. I did not eat for two days."

"But that is terrible! I will get you—" She stopped, suddenly at a loss. "I do not know what you eat."

"Rice, miss. Fish, maybe?"

"We do not have any fish. And I dare not cook rice; the cook would ask questions. I will bring you chicken and rolls and salad; eat what you can. And I will bring water, of course. And if you need to—that is, if you must—" She stopped again, defeated this time by propriety. How could she express, in words that Mr. Kee would understand, but without embarrassment—? "Ah." Her eyes lighted on an old, chipped chamber pot stacked atop other debris in one corner of the room. She pulled it down. "Do you know what this is?"

"Yes, miss." Surely there was a hint of a smile in his voice?

"Good." Her own voice held nothing but relief. "That is all, then. I will return soon with food and water."

"Miss?"

Hilda was on her way out of the room. She stopped and turned around; the candle flickered.

"Miss, you are very good Christian lady." His voice was unsteady. "I pray for you, miss."

"T'ank you," she said, her own eyes suddenly wet. Then she and her light went up the stairs.

Zeus does not bring all men's plans to fulfillment.

—Homer, *The Iliad*, c. 700 B.C.

y the time Hilda had foraged for food in the kitchen, prepared a plate for Mr. Kee, and taken it down to him along with a pitcher of water, she was weak from the tension. The other servants might be coming home at any moment. It was after seven. Though they didn't officially have to be back until nightfall, another hour at least, they might be tired, or hot, or hungry, or in need of the bathroom. *Herre Gud* alone knew *why* they would come, but come they would, and soon, and they mustn't catch her. She looked around apprehensively at every sound, and when her errand was finally completed, checked the laundry to make sure the visiting maid wasn't still there.

She had another worry, too. She had taken pity on Mr. Kee and left the candle with him after all, with strict instructions, repeated several times to make sure he understood, to extinguish it the very minute he finished his meal and not to light it again except in the direst of emergencies. It was against the most unbreakable rule of the household, but she had suddenly imagined herself alone and hunted, in a strange country, shut up far belowground in a strange house in pitch darkness, and she could not find it in her heart to do that to the poor little man. But she worried.

There are few physical activities that are as tiring as emotional excess. Hilda was sure, as she climbed the endless service stairs up to her room, that she felt a hundred years old. She could, she thought, fall asleep on her feet. And, in fact, some sleep now would be a good idea. She was going to be busy later tonight.

She dropped down onto her bed with a sigh, not even bothering to remove her boots. There were so many things to think about, so many plans to be made. She must work out a way to raise money for a ticket and get Mr. Kee safely on the train to Chicago. She must think how to find solid evidence of the judge's guilt. She must return a stolen will to a locked office, in the middle of the night.

That last was the problem she wanted least to think about, but she had to admit it was the most pressing of all. The law office would reopen for business first thing tomorrow morning, and the will must be back on Master James's desk long before that happened. She had made light of the difficulties when talking to Patrick, but she was apprehensive. In fact, she admitted to herself, she was downright scared, as they said in America.

Thinking of the slang word made her feel slightly better. She was good at the language. She was smart. She could do anything she wanted to.

What she could not do, apparently, was sleep. She took off her boots. She took off her clothes, right down to her chemise, for the room, with the sun pouring straight in the west window, was stifling. She washed herself in lukewarm water from the jug on the washstand, and let her body dry in the hot, still air before she lay down again. Nothing helped. Her imagination was too busy conjuring up the possible disasters that could overtake her in the next few days, if not this very night.

She was glad when she heard Norah plod up the stairs and enter the room next door. She knocked on the wall.

"Norah! Can you come here, please?"

"What for?" The voice sounded sulky.

"I wish to speak with you, and I cannot come out. I am not dressed."

"Hmph. Never bothered ye before." But after a moment or two Norah appeared in Hilda's doorway. "Saints preserve us! Ye meant 'not dressed,' didn't ye? Not hardly decent, ye're not."

"It is hot," said Hilda briefly. "Sit down. I need your help."

"Seems to me ye never talk to me lately but what ye want somethin'," Norah grumbled.

Hilda sat up, stung. "That is not true! You are my friend. Why are you in so bad a temper? This time I have done not'ing to you!"

Norah plunked herself down in the chair and made a face. "Sorry. Ye're right. It's not yer fault. It's that spalpeen of a Sean O'Neill I'm mad at! We watched the parade together, and then we took our picnic out to the river. That was all right. We were with some of his family, and some friends of his came and sat down near us, and we had a good time, laughin' and talkin' and—well, ye know."

Norah skipped judiciously over some of the rowdier bits. She knew that Hilda's stern Swedish conscience did not always approve of the goings-on in Norah's Irish crowd.

"And then, just as I was thinkin' it was time for Sean to walk me home, I looked around for him, and there he was, sittin' as bold as ye please with his cousin's neighbor, and she not more than half

Irish! A red-haired hussy, with skin like cream, and plenty of it showin', too. I could've gone and drowned in the river, for all he cared! So I brought meself home alone, and if Sean ever wants to take me out again, he'd better do some fancy talkin', I can tell ye."

Hilda had listened with scant patience; Norah's tales of woe with her gentlemen friends were too familiar to arouse much interest. She made appropriate noises of sympathy and understanding, however, until Norah had run down, and then she launched into her own story, starting with the part she thought would interest Norah most.

"Norah, there is trouble. I have much to do, and I do not know how to do all of it. I know who killed Miss Harper, and I know why, but I do not know how to prove it."

Sean was forgotten. "Who? Why? What? Tell me, quick!"

"It was Judge Harper, as I feared, but not for money. He has done something dishonest, and he has killed for fear it will come out!"

Norah gasped. "What has he done, then?"

"That," Hilda admitted, "is part of what I do not know, exactly." She rehearsed for Norah the scenario she and Patrick had worked out. "But to make the police take notice we must prove it, and I do not know how to do that. It is not a thing the servants would know, bribery and co—corr—"

"Corruption," Norah supplied with gleeful malice. "It shouldn't be so hard, Hilda. There's me cousin Ryan on the police force, ye know."

"*Ja-a,*" said Hilda, drawing the word out doubtfully. "But he is only a patrolman, and he would perhaps not know about wickedness in high places. I t'ink we need another politician, or a lawyer, or someone very important who can ask questions we cannot. And I do not know anyone important except Mr. Clem and Colonel George, and of course . . ."

She didn't have to complete the thought. Of course they couldn't ask their employers to investigate anything, certainly not the sins of an important member of their own party!

"If we knew a Democrat," Hilda began.

"Everybody we know is a Democrat," said Norah a trifle acidly. She had not liked the implication that her cousin on the police force was a nonentity.

"Yes, of course, everyone in our class, but we are not important people, Norah! I am sorry, you do not like me to say this, but we do not have the influence. We are only servants and laborers. No one will pay attention to us. No one will tell us secret things. We need a Democrat who can ask questions, who knows people—oh!"

Her eyes began to dance.

"The *newspaper*, Norah! The *Times*!"

"Oh, yeah? What about it?" She was still surly, but Hilda didn't notice.

"We will go to the *Times* and tell them the story, and they will send people to ask questions. They know important people, and they will want to help us because they are a Democratic publication and the judge is a Republican—oh, it is a beautiful idea! We have used the newspapers once, to help make Mr. Kee safe, and—oh, Norah, that is the other thing! I almost forgot. We have Mr. Kee!"

Norah was jolted out of her sulks completely. She listened avidly while Hilda explained.

"Well, me girl," she said when Hilda had finished, "that's somethin' we can do, all us 'unimportant' people. No, don't apologize again. I know what ye mean, all right, when I'm in me right temper. But it's people like us, poor people, who'll help another poor man. If ye think he'll be safe till, say, tomorrow afternoon, I'll bet ye anything ye like I'll have him aboard the train."

She looked like the cat that swallowed the canary. Hilda eyed her doubtfully.

"You can raise the money so quickly? But we do not know even how much the ticket will cost, and we do not have time enough to talk to many people in less than one day."

"I've got to talk to only one person, one o' them unimportant people," Norah said with a broad grin. "One of me cousins is a conductor on the Lake Shore and Michigan Southern!"

"May *Herre Gud* bless big Irish families!" said Hilda fervently.

They made plans. Mr. Kee had to have clothes; he could not keep Patrick's.

"Ye say he's short. How short?"

Hilda considered. "Shorter than you, but only a little. Maybe . . ." She measured with her fingers.

"Too tall for me little brother's clothes, then."

"What about your sister?"

"Me sister! Why'd a Chinaman want to go around in a girl's clothes?"

"I do not think he will want to, but it will be better, maybe. The police, they look for a man, not a woman. And he has a braid of hair down his back. It does not look like a man's hair, an American man. If we pulled it up around the top of his head, and gave him a skirt . . . *ja?*"

"Got it!" Norah was getting into the spirit of this. "Katie, she's got an old skirt that would maybe do. He isn't fat, is he? I think I'd better see him."

But this Hilda firmly refused to let Norah do. "Someone might see you. Me, I must go down tonight to tell him the plans, and that is enough. If anyone knew he was here . . ." There was real terror in her voice, and Norah acceded, somewhat unwillingly.

"I'll see him when he goes to the train, then, but I just hope the clothes fit."

"He is not at all fat," Hilda assured her. "Patrick is not a big man, but his clothes make Mr. Kee look like a child."

They agreed that Norah would go first thing in the morning to get the clothes and then talk to her cousin at the train station, Hilda covering for her at Tippecanoe Place if anyone noticed her absence.

"But I will let you out a window, early, before anyone is out of bed. There is a kitchen window that is good for to get out when the house is locked." She grinned at Norah. "I know, you see. I tell you all, later. But, Norah, there is one more thing." The grin disappeared.

"*Now* what?"

Hilda was unusually hesitant. She paused to choose her words carefully. "I do not like to ask you. You do much for me already. But there is no one else who is so good a friend."

"All right, ye've got me buttered up nicely. Spit it out!"

"It is the will. Tonight, late, late, when everyone has come home and gone to bed, I must return it. Patrick cannot come; he must work. And I do not want to go alone. Not at night. I—I am afraid."

"It's about time ye showed some sense, me girl! If yer precious Patrick can't come with ye, ye can bet I will. And happy ye're lettin' me in on the fun at last!"

26

To him who is in fear everything rustles.

—Sophocles, *Acrisius*,
fifth century B.C.

hey slept a little once the sun had gone down and their rooms were cooler. Hilda had suggested a snack, so they had made a giggling raid on the kitchen once Mrs. Sullivan was safely home, in bed and snoring. Leftover fried chicken and chocolate cake had begun to make them sleepy, and when Hilda had made a quick visit to the cellar and found Mr. Kee peacefully asleep (with the candle safely blown out), she decided she would talk to him early in the morning. For now she could relax into a nap.

When she woke, the house was dark and still. Lighting a forbidden match, she looked at the alarm clock, which told her it was five past two, far later than she had intended to sleep. She made an annoyed noise and got out of bed.

The room was very dark. Hilda felt her way to the window and peered out. She could see no stars, but she could hear a restless wind, and there was a heaviness to the air. Another storm was coming up.

She dared not knock on the wall to wake Norah, so she dressed quickly and stole out of her room, opening Norah's door.

"Norah," she whispered. The sound was barely audible even to her, and Norah's quiet breathing continued undisturbed. "Norah! Wake up!"

Nothing.

In desperation she went into the room and reached out for where she imagined Norah's arm to be, to give it a shake.

"Oo-ooh!"

The shivery sound seemed to Hilda as loud as a scream. Her aim had been faulty. She removed her hand from Norah's face quickly and moved it to her shoulder. "Sshh!" she urged in a frantic whisper. "It is only me! You must get up, please, and *be quiet!*"

Once she was awake, Norah was efficient. She was up and dressed in a few minutes. Like Hilda, she dispensed with her stays and simply put on a black uniform dress with as little on underneath as decency allowed.

Hilda went back to her own room, armed herself with her makeshift lock picks and the will, and together the two girls tiptoed down the service stairs, taking care to keep to the outside edges of the treads to avoid squeaks.

Hilda had climbed onto a chair and was trying to open the kitchen window quietly when Norah said, "Wait!"

"Do not do that to me! I nearly fell! What is it? Did you hear something?"

"No. Sorry. But we need a light."

"Oh." Hilda climbed down. "I did not think of that."

"It's pitch black out there, me girl, and what'll it be like inside the office?"

"Yes. You are right. I will get a candle."

"We need light on the street, too," Norah objected. "And it's far too windy out there for a candle. Best we get a dark lantern, so we don't stick out like a lighthouse. There's one down cellar; I can get it in two ticks."

"No, you will not go down there. I will get a candle," said Hilda firmly.

Norah sighed. It had been worth a try.

Hilda got out the kitchen window with less difficulty this time; practice makes perfect. She was also, to some degree, prepared for the cold nose on her ankle.

"Quiet, Rex! Good dog."

"Ouch!" This from Norah, who had just scrambled out and scraped her shin. "Drat that railing! What's that dog doing here?"

"He likes me, I think. He came to me before, when I was out at night."

The conversation was conducted in stifled whispers as the two girls climbed the stairs and moved away from the house, walking on the grass to muffle their footsteps.

"Huh! Just lonesome, that's what's the matter with him. What'll we do if he tries to come with us?"

Hilda considered. Rex was trotting along happily by her side.

"I t'ink—I *think* I will let him come. He knows to be quiet, and it might be good . . ."

"Hmm. Mebbe ye're right. A dog can come in handy if . . ."

They might not voice their fears, but both knew exactly what the other was thinking. Secretly each was passionately glad of the dog's comforting presence.

"We go this way." Hilda pointed south on Taylor Street, which they had now reached. Her voice was low, but she no longer bothered to whisper. They were well away from the house.

"Why?" demanded Norah. "The office is straight up Washington, and there aren't as many streetlights on Jefferson."

"There are no streetlights on Jefferson. They turn those off at midnight. That is why we go that way," said Hilda.

"Oh." Norah gulped. "I told you we should have a lantern."

The walk had not seemed long to Hilda, twelve hours or so ago in the middle of a sunlit afternoon. In the middle of a pitch-black, windy night it dragged on endlessly. The wind tried to hurry them, pushing against their backs and making them stumble as obstacles rose out of the dark. Overhead it lashed at the trees, making the boughs creak and the leaves hiss furiously. The two girls could see almost nothing except at corners, where a little light reached them from the arc lamps a block away, and they could hear almost nothing over the tumult of the wind. Anyone could be following them. Any*thing* could be.

Hilda, who was always a little afraid of trees and their spirits, reached her hand out to Norah's. Clinging to one another like children, they toiled on.

"I think we are here." Hilda had to raise her voice to be heard. "I have counted corners. This alley should lead to the building. Ah, it is not so windy here."

The narrow alley, with buildings on either side, protected them a little from the tempest and its noise. "Here," said Hilda, "if you will hold the candle, I will try to light the match, so we can see . . . " She swore as the match was blown out.

After three tries, she gave up. "It is no use. I will soon have no matches left. We are at the right place, or we are not. I can tell by touch, I think, when we are nearer. There should be a staircase . . . here . . ." Her questing hands reached out for the darker shade of black looming ahead and felt the rough wooden uprights that supported the railing.

"It is here. Now we climb and see if it is the right one."

"What if it isn't?" Norah was trying to keep the fear from

her voice, and was not succeeding very well. Rex, still their faithful escort, whined softly. Only Norah heard him.

"If it is not, then we try again. Perhaps we will have to go to the front of the buildings, to Washington Street. It will not matter so much here, the lights. We are far from the judge's house."

Norah swallowed hard, but followed Hilda up the steps. Rex, hating the open staircase but unwilling to be left behind, brought up the rear.

They were not forced into the streetlit prominence of Washington Street after all. Hilda had found the right building, and the commodious back window was still unlocked. The lock picks weren't going to be needed.

It was much quieter inside the building. Norah scrambled in the window after Hilda, lifted Rex inside, and closed the window. "For he's a good dog to come with us, and I'll not leave him out there where it's goin' to storm any minute."

She spoke in a whisper. There was no need to do so in a deserted building, but it seemed somehow wiser.

Hilda lit the candle. The flame flickered and danced against the ceiling-high stacks of boxes; the window rattled in its frame. Norah shuddered and moved even closer to Hilda than the small space required.

"Now. Hold the candle. The key is here." She opened the key box and motioned to Norah to hold the candle closer. "But— it should be on this hook—Norah, it is gone!"

"So ye can't get in?"

"I can get in, yes. I can pick the lock, as I did before. But this is bad, Norah! It means someone has been here, after I left, and has been in Mr. James's office. It was not Mr. James; he would have his own key and would not need this one."

"Mebbe he lost it," offered Norah. "Drinkin' like he does, he could lose somethin', easy."

"It is possible," Hilda agreed doubtfully. "But I fear that someone else has been here, someone who has no business here, perhaps even the judge. And that could mean that he has looked for the will, and knows that it is gone, and—"

"And knows now who took it," said the voice out of the darkness, with an entirely unpleasant laugh. "And knows what to do with meddling servant girls who can't keep their mouths shut!"

Mrs. Harper, a lantern in her hand, stood in the doorway. To Hilda, the smile on her face looked like the rictus of a skull.

Each person is born to one possession which outvalues all the others—his last breath.

—Mark Twain, *Following the Equator*, 1897

ou!" said Hilda. "But I thought—"

"You thought it was Judge Harper, didn't you? You thought he was the one who killed her for her money, before she could will it away to some stupid mission or church or charity? Oh, no, my dear. My beloved husband thinks honor is more important than money. He sees himself in Washington, righting the country's wrongs. Never mind that his wife has to scrimp and save and make do with last year's gowns and no butler! Never mind that his son has so little to come and go on that he's taken to drink from the shame of it! No, money isn't important, not for him!"

Her voice dripped with scorn. "Someone had to save the

money. Someone had to save us from ruin. And I'll not have you interfering. It isn't healthy to interfere."

"Is that the reason you killed Wanda—because she interfered?" The question was meaningless, but every moment that Hilda could keep her talking was another moment to live.

"You know it is. She found the rest of that wretched ivory comb, found it in our backyard where I killed that wretched woman. I'd hunted for it, but couldn't find it all by moonlight."

"Oh, so that's what you were looking for!" Even in this moment of extreme danger Hilda was relieved to know that she had seen a real person that terrible night, not a ghost.

"You saw me, did you? If I'd known that, I'd have disposed of you earlier. There are too many eyes," she said discontentedly. "That stupid Wanda didn't even know what she'd found, but came to me to ask if she might keep the pretty thing! If anyone else had seen it, and asked where she'd found it—but no matter, now."

She moved a step closer to the terrified girls. "I'll thank you to give me that will. If you thought you could prove something with it, you're wrong. And now you'll never tell, will you?"

Hilda shivered despite the heat of the room. She had never heard so cold a voice.

"It's a pity you had to involve your friend here," Mrs. Harper went on. She nodded at Norah, who was cringing against the window. "She'll have to go, too, but I'll blame it all on that ridiculous little Chinaman. Oh, yes, my dear, I know where he is. One of those visiting maids in that fine house you work in figured it out, and she told Annie. But morning will do to take care of that little problem. Now give me the will!"

"But—but you are wrong!" Hilda couldn't help it. "The will is not what you think. The money—it goes to the church. It was always to go to the church, it—"

"You lie! Give it to me!"

Mrs. Harper's voice had risen to a screech. Numbly, Hilda reached in the bosom of her dress for the will, and then several things happened at once.

As Hilda drew out the will, Mrs. Harper lunged for it. Rex, who had been growing more unhappy by the moment, sprang to protect his friend and buried his teeth in Mrs. Harper's ankle. She screamed, dropping her lantern at the same moment Norah's elbow knocked over a stack of boxes.

In her frantic effort to dislodge the dog, Mrs. Harper kicked over the lantern. The kerosene spilled onto the floor and began to soak the boxes.

"Rex! No! Rex, *stop!* It is dangerous. The fumes—"

The dog unwillingly loosed his hold, wriggled under a fallen box, and came whining to Hilda.

"Norah, the window! We must get out! Here, take the dog!"

Norah, her teeth chattering, opened the window, dumped Rex outside, and prepared to climb out herself, with Hilda right behind her.

As Norah struggled with her skirts, she dropped her candle and watched with horrified fascination as the flame ignited the dry cardboard of the nearest box and began to lick toward the pool of kerosene.

Mrs. Harper screamed again, but before she could get past the boxes, the crawling worm of fire had reached the next box— the one that was soaked from the fallen lamp. With a roar that was almost an explosion, the deadly combination of the volatile fuel and the angry wind coming through the window shot up in flames nearly to the ceiling. Mrs. Harper's clothing was burning in an instant.

The blast knocked the two girls out the window, but Hilda turned to go back.

"Hilda! Hilda, don't! Are ye out of yer mind, girl?"

"I must help her—Mrs. Harper, she will die—"

"She's a murderess, Hilda, and there's nothin' ye can do, anyway. Come *away!*"

With the strength imparted by fear, Norah dragged the taller girl down the flimsy stairs, which were already beginning to smolder. Poor Rex, torn between his terror of the fire and his terror of the stairs, was the last one down, and Norah had to beat out the sparks on his coat.

IN THE FEW minutes it took Hilda to run to the corner and operate the alarm box, the flames raged hungrily over the second floor of the building and began to spread to the third. By the time the fire trucks arrived, bells clanging, there was great danger of the fire spreading to the adjacent building. Fire Chief Kerner, along with Patrick and his fellow firemen, managed to prevent that disaster, aided by the heavy rain that finally came, but the law offices of Harper, Hill, Brookins, and Harper, along with the other businesses in the building, were gone forever.

A cool dawn was about to break when Hilda, Norah, and Patrick walked up the back drive of Tippecanoe Place. All were soaked to the skin and exhausted; all smelled of smoke. No one spoke. In a few stolen moments during the terrible night, Hilda had explained to Patrick. Now there seemed to be nothing to say, until they reached the kitchen stairs. Then Patrick spoke.

"I'll make sure Mr. Williams knows everything. Don't worry." Everyone at Tippecanoe Place—servants, family, guests, and all, except for poor Mr. Kee, alone and terrified in the cellar—had turned up at the fire scene, at least for a few minutes. Mr. Williams had been horrified to find Norah and Hilda there, faces black with smoke and streaked with tears, but a partial explanation had pacified him. Still somewhat bewildered, he had promised to leave the back door unlocked for them, and had taken Rex home.

"I am sorry, Patrick." Hilda was crying, the tears of utter exhaustion. Neither she nor anyone else noticed.

"It wasn't your fault, me girl. I'm only glad both of you lived to tell the tale. I'll come to see you this afternoon when we've both had some sleep."

The two girls slept until mid-afternoon, then woke only because the sun shone in their west windows, bright and hot. Hilda, shocked by the time, washed and dressed quickly in her uniform and went next door to Norah.

She, too, had just dressed. "And can ye imagine them lettin' us sleep this late? How do ye feel?"

"Awful," said Hilda. "My eyes sting. And I wish I could wash my hair. I do not think I will ever get the smell of smoke out of it."

"Me neither. Well, girl, we'd best get downstairs and see if we still have jobs."

"Oh, I cannot even think of it!" Hilda rolled her eyes and followed Norah down the stairs.

When they reached the servants' lounge, it was evident that very little work was being done that day. The entire staff, with the exception of Mr. Williams, was present and in animated conversation, which stopped short as the two girls entered.

Mrs. Sullivan was the one who broke the silence.

"Mr. Williams wants to see you, the both of you. The minute you came down, he said. He's in the butler's pantry." She nodded toward the door.

At these ominous words Hilda and Norah looked at each other and gulped, but they headed straight for the pantry; they dared not delay.

Mr. Williams was cleaning the silver. "Ah, there you are. I trust you slept well after your—er—harrowing experience?"

"Yes, sir," murmured Hilda faintly. "Thank you, sir."

The butler put down his polishing cloth. "Shall we repair to a more—er—private place? There is no one in the breakfast room at present."

He pointed to the door on the other side of the pantry, which led to the dining room the family used when they had no guests. Its small, intimate table would seat no more than twelve.

Mr. Williams gestured to the two girls to sit. They placed themselves gingerly on the very edge of two chairs; the butler took a third.

"Well." He cleared his throat. "This is a most—er— unusual situation."

"Yes, sir," said Hilda, since some reply seemed called for.

"I must tell you that considerable discussion has taken place while you slept."

This time neither girl said a word, but their nerves tightened.

"Mr. Cavanaugh explained to me in detail what happened. I may say, Hilda, that your actions appear to me to have been foolhardy in the extreme, not to mention their being in absolute violation of every rule of this house. However"—he held up his hand as Hilda opened her mouth—"I am prepared to accept the notion that your motives were good. I have spoken with both Mr. and Mrs. Studebaker."

Two pairs of eyes were fixed on his.

"They are inclined to be relieved that the question of the murders has been resolved, and to be grateful for your part, Hilda, in their resolution. They wish, of course, that the end result had been less tragic."

"I, too, wish that," said Hilda quietly.

"Yes. Well. Perhaps, in a way, the fire was just as well. Justice was served, and in a quicker, more merciful way than that administered by the state. Now."

He cleared his throat. "We have decided that your part in the matter—both of you, Hilda and Norah—should be—er—handled discreetly. We would rather have this household connected with the matter as tenuously as possible. The two of you were at the fire scene, of course, rather too prominently. That fact cannot be denied. Therefore, Mrs. Studebaker suggested that perhaps Rex smelled the fire, became excited and went to investigate, and that you two went after him, unfortunately becoming slightly burned in the process of rescuing him. That is the story that we have given to the newspapers, and we trust you will agree to it."

His tone made it clear that disagreement was not an option.

"Yes, sir," said Hilda, and Norah nodded. "That could be what happened."

"Very well. That is what you will say to the other servants, or to anyone else who may ask. You are relieved of your duties for today, but I will expect you to resume them in the usual fashion tomorrow. Meanwhile, Judge Harper would like you, Hilda, to call on him at four o'clock."

"The judge? He wishes me to visit him?"

"That is what he said. He will be at home. And may I suggest," added Mr. Williams, his nose wrinkling slightly, "that you take the time to wash thoroughly and change all your clothing before you go? And perhaps this evening both of you should wash your hair."

"Yes, sir," said Norah, with just the hint of a smile. "Sir?"
"Yes?"

"I hope Rex is all right, sir. He—he saved our lives, ye know."

The butler's expression softened slightly. "He is in good health and spirits, barring some singed hair. He, too, will require frequent bathing for the next few days. Thank you for asking, Norah. He is an excellent dog. That is all, then."

"Excuse me, sir," said Hilda, her mouth dry. "There is one other thing. Do you know—I mean, has anyone told you— I have done something that you may not—"

Norah grew impatient. "What she's tryin' to say, sir, is has anybody told you about the Chinaman in the cellar?"

"Ah, yes, Mr. Kee." Mr. Williams's voice was wintry. "We shall have to discuss your predilection for the flouting of rules, Hilda. However, again, your motives appear to have been sound. Mr. Cavanaugh told me about the unfortunate man, and Mr. Studebaker has taken care of the matter. The manager of the Studebaker Repository in Chicago knows some members of the Chinese community there. Mr. Kee has been dispatched to his care."

"How about that, then?" said Norah when they were safely out in the hall. "We've found out a murderess and rescued a Chinaman and kept our jobs, as well!"

"But I must still speak to the judge," muttered Hilda darkly.

When in doubt tell the truth.

—Mark Twain, *Following
the Equator*, 1897

I t was four o'clock on the dot when Hilda, as clean and tidy
as possible, presented herself at the house next door and rang
the bell. The judge himself answered the door.

"I have given the servants a few days off," he said in answer
to Hilda's look of surprise. "Please come in."

They sat in the parlor, the judge hardly less stiffly than Hilda.
He said nothing for a time, and Hilda couldn't bear the silence.

"Please, I wish to say I am very sorry, sir—Your Honor—
Judge Harper—"

"I have resigned from the bench," he said. " 'Mr. Harper'
will do. There is no need to apologize, Miss Johansson. This was
none of your doing."

He sighed heavily. "I knew what she had done, of course. I
knew from the first. She was always fond of money, and she was

not happy when I left the law practice. I felt there was nothing else I could do. How could I continue to have a financial interest in a firm whose lawyers might appear in my court? But she was bitter about it."

He studied his hands. "This is all my fault, really. I knew about Mary's—Miss Harper's—will. I helped her draw it up years ago, and when she came home and told me she wished to change it, to remove my children as beneficiaries since they were now well established, I agreed that it was a sound decision. Of course I didn't tell my wife; it was a confidential matter. I had no idea she thought all the money was coming to me, but I ought to have known. I ought to have provided a better income for her."

"But, sir," Hilda burst out, "you cannot blame yourself for what she did. She was—she was a little mad, I think."

"Yes." The judge sounded infinitely tired. "And perhaps I could not have prevented her killing Mary. But the next death—I could have stopped that. And she nearly killed you and your friend. If I had had the courage to go to the police—but I had not that courage. It would have ruined my political career, and I thought that I could do some real good." His voice had grown bitter. "I have given up politics now, of course. It will all come out. My family and I will have to weather the storm as best we may."

He rose; Hilda got to her feet as well. "I asked you to come here so that I could assure you I hold you in no blame. You acted with great courage and intelligence."

He held out his hand, and after a stunned moment, Hilda took it. "I will not see you again, Miss Johansson. I will sell this house and leave South Bend. My son will, I think, be all right on his own, now that . . ." He did not finish the sentence. "Good-bye. I believe you will go far."

Hilda curtsied. "Good-bye, sir. I hope . . ." But she could not find words. There was little hope in Judge Harper's future. "I will see myself out, sir."

And she walked across the lawn to the great house next door. As she neared the gate between the two properties, she saw Patrick, sitting on the bench by the carriage house. Her steps quickened.

"Oh, Patrick! I have much to tell you!"

AFTERWORD

Merely corroborative detail, intended to give artistic
verisimilitude to an otherwise bald and unconvincing narrative.
—William S. Gilbert,
The Mikado, 1885

The woman who gave Hilda the lemonade found Patrick as
charming as he intended her to, and when she read the
newspaper story of Mrs. Harper and the murders, she treasured the glass forever afterward as her souvenir of the most
exciting events of her lifetime.

Mr. Kee found a refuge in Chicago's Chinatown, wrote to
Father Zahm and recovered his few belongings, and eventually
opened a very successful restaurant.

Largely owing to Mr. Williams's patriotic love of Gilbert
and Sullivan, Patrick was able to secure his permission to take
Hilda to a matinee of *The Mikado* at the grand Oliver Opera
House. She wore a new hand-me-down from Mrs. George, very

fine in navy blue and hydrangea, and would have enjoyed herself even more if her stays had not been laced so tightly she could scarcely breathe.

On June 4, 1900, Father Zahm celebrated the twenty-fifth anniversary of his ordination with a special mass at the Church of the Sacred Heart on the Notre Dame campus. A serenade by the university band followed, then an elaborate dinner. Among the guests were Mr. Clement and Mr. J. M. Studebaker.

On June sixth, the front page of the South Bend *Tribune* reported "War Clouds in China." A gunboat and two battleships were dispatched.

On June ninth, a large picture of Mr. Clem Studebaker graced the front page of the *Tribune*, accompanying a two-page story about the new Milburn Memorial Methodist Episcopal Church he and his wife were about to build.

On June twenty-first, Jacob Kerner, the popular fire chief, saved the life of an infant trapped on the third floor of a burning hotel. The chief signaled to the injured and distraught parents to throw the child down to him—and caught him, unharmed.

In the November election of 1900, the Honorable Abraham Brick was returned by a handsome majority to his second term as representative from Indiana's Thirteenth Congressional District. He was to have a distinguished career in the House for the next eight years until his death in office.